Eclipsed Imprint

Belle Hale

ISBN-13: 978-0-9953924-5-8
ISBN-10: 0995392455

For my mother; the strongest woman I know

"She slept with wolves without fear, for the wolves knew a lion was among them."

R.M. Drake

ACKNOWLEDGMENTS

As always, I would like to thank God for His unwaivering love and guidance; for holding me up when I am weak, and for always giving me a safe place to fall when I feel at my lowest. I can't thank Him enough for the myriad of prosperity and the endless blessings He has placed in my life.

To my wolf pack, your continued love, encouragement, excitement, and patience with my lack of housework and home cooked meals during this creative process is above and beyond what I deserve, but cherished in the deepest form. I love each of you more than anything in the entire existence of the universe, and I hope I make you as proud as you each make me every single day.

My most heartfelt thanks goes out to my parents for their unconditional love, and for their honest constructive criticism; not only about my work but also about life in general. I don't know where I would be if it wasn't for their guiding light.

I must also thank my extended family and friends for their loyalty, love, and for being my biggest supporters not only in regards to my work, but also in life and when I need them the most.

To the winner of the Eclipsed Imprint title competition and my dear friend, Nat, thank you for your unwaivering love, friendship and support.

To my wonderful readers and followers worldwide, I send my most sincere thanks for the warm reception Soul Imprint received, and for the lovely messages I receive on a daily basis from so many of you. There aren't words to describe how grateful I am for your kindness and support. I hope Eclipsed Imprint is received half as successfully as Soul Imprint was. Thank you from the bottom of my heart, and happy reading.

An extra special shout out to the following loyal readers: Laci Conde, Linda Levine, Crystal Watson, Jamie Magnusson, Julie Haggard, Angela McMasters, Jen Zingaro, Melissa Mendoza, Kelly Ryder, and Jackie Wright. You ladies are beyond beautiful and such a blast to talk to. Thank you for all the fun!

I

∞

I opened my eyes and found myself lost in the deep tawny gaze of my fiancé staring back at me. How could life get any better than this? I was in the arms of the man I am to marry in less than twelve hours, and I am surrounded by his love, his beauty, his scent; him. He is mine and I am his, and despite what some may think, there was nothing anyone could do to take him away from me. Roman's lips curl in at the corners as he watches me, his bare chest hovering over mine, his eyes drinking me in.

It didn't matter that he looked at me like this on an hourly basis, or that he told me how beautiful I was whenever he got the chance; I could never understand his reasoning or see what he saw. He watched me as if I was the most spectacular thing he had ever laid eyes on; he breathed me in as if I provided the air he needed to live. I could relate when it came to him, but it was different for me somehow.

Our eyes locked as he heard my thoughts—another thing I would never be able to get used to. Roman lowered his body to mine, his hands guiding my face up to his.

"I miss you already," he breathed, his warm hands smoothing over my hair.

"Not as much as I miss you," I sulked.

Roman chuckled silently as our lips touched. His summer-warm smile slowly fading. I lightly traced my fingertips over his fading smile wondering what was wrong.

"Uncle Red is here. It's almost time for me to go," he murmured, sadness saturating his tone. My arms automatically locked around his waist, crushing him against my body. A light tremble rippled through him, and our lips met once more.

Roman let out a contented sigh as he gently pulled away.

"Maybe you could sneak back in through the window tonight? Nobody would need to know," I smiled a devilish smile. I thought he would be all for the idea, or smile at the very least, but he didn't, he simply looked at me as if I had two heads.

"*We will know*," he murmured in a low tone. "As much as I know we both hate the thought of being apart, this is tradition, and I'm not anything if not traditional," his sweet breath washed over my lips.

He started to pull away and in a panic I tightened my grip around him, hugging myself to his solid-stone body.

"Wait," I demanded desperately. "What if… what if we make a new tradition? Our own tradition?" I knew I was grasping at straws; there was no way he would break *tradition*.

He chuckled then, easing himself back down so that our bodies were touching again.

"No," he said with a grin.

I rolled my eyes, scoffing with disappointment. Roman interlaced our fingers, a flirtatious—no—a *suspicious* gleam in his eyes.

"What are you worried I'll do when I leave here tonight?" he asked, a hint of suspicion echoing through his husky voice.

I feigned ignorance, like I had no idea what he was talking about.

"Elle. I know you better than you know yourself. Give it up,"

My eyes narrowed at his perfectly bright white smile. I didn't understand why he asked half the questions he did, I mean, he could get inside my head and abduct my thoughts any time he wanted.

I swept my tongue over my bottom lip as I suppressed a smile. I knew he heard me; his lips twitched in that way and I was at his mercy.

"Ugh, fine… I know the sorts of things

men do on their last night of freedom… and I'm not sure I like the idea of my husband being involved in such distasteful behavior,"

"Really?" he murmured in a low tone. I lift my eyebrows in reply and Roman chuckles silently, shaking his head.

"What on earth makes you think that *I* would want to be involved in something like *that*?" he stared at me questioningly, his eyes softening as he watched me battling to find the answer to his fair question.

I shrug, an apologetic smile touching my lips. Roman's features slowly become serious, his stare fixed on mine.

"Listen to me… I will never, nor have I ever had any interest in the sleazy, immature, degrading, and stereotypical bachelor night nonsense. Those sorts of parties are thrown by perverted jocks who regret that their single lives are coming to an end. I, however, am very much looking forward to becoming a married man." His voice is low and breathy.

"You are, are you?" I ask speculatively.

Roman nods, his lips inching closer to

mine.

"And why is that Mr. Kahoa?"

"So I can hear you call me your husband over and over again, Mrs. Kahoa," the corner of his mouth lifted into his crooked smile.

"That's Miss Taylor to you, Mr. Kahoa," I tease playfully.

"Until tomorrow," he reminds me, forever in his eyes.

"Hmm." I close my eyes, content to lay in the shrouded darkness with Roman surrounding me. He strokes my hair.

"Stop worrying," he scolds, gentle as ever.

"I'm not," I murmur, my brows knitting together.

"Ella," he warns.

"Roman," I prod back, opening one eye to peek up at him. He smiles his sweetest smile, his eyes radiating mirth, melting my heart into a puddle of pre-wedding goo. How lucky I am to be marrying this wonderfully beautiful man.

"Cheeky as ever," he presses his lips

firmly on my hair.

We are both startled by a heavy knock at the door. Roman orders whoever it is away, snapping something in Qaletaqa and turns his attention back to me.

"Do you have everything you need?" I ask, feeling his departure looming over us. Roman nods hesitantly, glancing at his packed suitcase sitting by the door, his stare seemingly far away.

"What are you thinking about?"

Roman subtly shakes his head and turns his gaze back to mine.

"About tomorrow… I know it will be difficult for you,"

My brow furrowed as the reality behind Roman's words burned through the imaginary shield I had so gravely enclosed my heart in. The aftermath of losing my parents impacted my daily life on an unimaginable level. Roman was the only person I allowed close enough to know how severely I was struggling without them. He was so gentle with my heart, and so incredibly patient with all of my shortcomings—not that he saw them as shortcomings, of course.

"Would you like me here when you read your mom's letter?" Roman's velvety voice guided me back to the now.

I shook my head gingerly, still questioning my answer. A soft smile floated on Roman's lips as his eyes watched me with deep concentration.

"No, it's okay. I can do it on my own…" I smiled an assuring smile, though I didn't quite feel the conviction behind my words.

"My brave girl," he stared lovingly into my eyes, his expression content. "You make me so proud, Elle." Roman entwined us together, his lips blazing against the hollow of my throat. We stayed like that for a long moment, savoring how it felt to be wrapped up in each other's arms.

Later, maintaining tradition, the time had come for Roman to leave for the night. The most indescribable pain mutilated my heart, and for what reason, I wasn't sure. Being apart from him would hurt, I knew this, and it was for that very reason that I had decided I would lock myself away in our room the moment he was gone. I didn't want to be around anyone if I couldn't be around him, and it wasn't like I would be of any use to anyone anyway; this pain was unbearable, so much so that I was contemplating another shot at persuading Roman to sneak back in to be with me tonight. The pain I was feeling now was so unfamiliar, so different to anything I'd ever felt before; there was an urgency behind it—it scared me.

Roman said his goodbyes to the family and we slowly made our way out to Uncle Red's truck.

The deep blue sky radiated above us, a thousand sparkling stars shined brightly, bathing us in their brilliant light as we stood in each other's arms for the final time tonight.

He wrapped his arms around my body. "Tomorrow you will be mine forever." Roman whispered as his hand ran down my spine, stopping at the small of my back.

"I am already yours forever," I reminded

him, referring to our eternal connection. I sensed his smile.

"Indeed you are." He hugs me tightly, then pulls away to watch me. "How incredibly lucky I am," he caresses my face softly, and leans in, touching his lips to mine.

"I love you, Miss Taylor," he grins coyly.

I smile. "I love you, Mr. Kahoa."

And after one more intense moment enveloped in his arms, Roman bends, grasping his suitcase and places it in the bed of the truck. He kisses the back of my hand before climbing into the backseat and I watch helplessly as he drives away, his eyes offering a silent plea. *Inside.* I hear the faded echo that is Roman's request as the taillights disappear into the dusky tunnel of trees, and I comply, starting inside.

Once inside and thinking I had successfully dodged my new family, Nova surprised me when I entered our room and flicked on the light.

"Gah! Nova! What the hell are you doing sitting here in the dark?" I scowled, trying to breathe through my mini-heart-attack.

Her eyes dance with amusement before an apologetic smile imprints her lips. "Sorry, Elle. It's just I knew you were trying to avoid everyone tonight but I wanted to spend some time with you before you went to sleep," she sounded hopeful, and her shoulders were raised in that way where she appeared to be holding her breath. Damn it. I didn't have the heart to turn her away.

I sighed, feeling defeated. "Okay... but only you!" I warned.

Nova's eyes lit up, her shoulders dipped—essentially releasing the breath she was holding—and she crushed me in her almighty wolf-strength hug as she squealed excitedly, lifting my mood slightly.

"Have you decided how you're going to wear your hair?" she asked as she released her bone crushing hold.

"Not really, but, I thought about maybe curling my hair and, you know, wearing them out loosely?" it was a question. This would normally be a decision Lena would be perfect to enquire about with; all of my wedding day decisions would have included my mom's input if she wasn't...

Nova's hand clasped around mine, stealing my attention.

"Hey, that's a great idea. And I'm sure one Lena would have chosen, too," Nova smiles, her eyes kind. I nod, needing to agree with her.

"Go take a shower and I'll meet you back here in about an hour, okay?"

My body tenses at the thought of being left alone again, though, I know Nova understands I need a moment, and I'm grateful. She hugs me as gently as she can before gliding gracefully out of the room.

I make my way into our bathroom, and fidget with the tap until I have the exact water temperature I want. The entire room fills with a mist of steam as I undress and step into the sweltering stream of water, and curl into a ball on the tiled shower floor. I wail, howling like a wolf crying at a full-moon; releasing all of my bottled-up pain, anguish and grief. I lay there for an unknown amount of time, but decide to crawl out once the hot water begins to fade.

Nova is waiting for me when I emerge from the bathroom wrapped in Roman's robe.

"How do you feel?" she asks, sitting on the edge of the bed, her cautious eyes watching me intently.

I shrug my shoulders, unsure of my answer. Nova smiles, and pats the empty space in front of her. "Come," she murmurs.

I oblige, sitting on the bed, my back to her. "You said you wanted curls," she holds up a small clear bag of curlers. I can't stifle the smile that curls my lips. "What?" she asks as she rakes a comb through my knotted hair.

"Aren't they just a little bit… I don't know… retro?"

Nova chuckles. "They get the job done, okay?"

"Okay," I raise my hands in surrender.

We sit in silence as Nova rolls my hair

around different sized curlers and fastens them to my skull. My mind wanders, thinking of what Roman is doing in that exact moment. I hear a faint murmur in the back of my mind, I steady my breathing and I focus. *Stop worrying.* I hear him say, an edge to his tone. I smile. Oh, my eavesdropping wolfy, always in my head. *I'm not worrying, Mr. Wolf, I was simply wondering what you were doing while I am being subjected to pre-wedding beauty torture by your sister.* Roman chuckles darkly in my mind, his laugh music to my ears. *I would pay to see that.* I hear his smile, and it compels mine. *I'm sure you would. Now, go away, you're no help.* I sulk. Roman chuckles quietly once more. *Until tomorrow, my love.* He breathes.

And all goes quiet for a prolonged moment, until I am surrounded by the sound of my wolf howling in the distance. He's here. He's been here the whole time. My heart warms and it takes every ounce of strength I have not to go running into the night to find him.

My head is throbbing from how tight Nova has secured the curlers to my skull. I am almost forced to pull them all out and just settle for curling my hair the normal way people do it in this century, but Nova is one step ahead of me, these curlers aren't budging the slightest, they only cause me more agony the more I try to loosen them— Gah! I give up.

Now alone, my eyes wander to the bookshelf where the handcrafted wooden memory box Roman made for my birthday sits staring back at me. It's now or never, I think to myself as I question whether to pull it down or not. The letters my mom wrote to me are inside, one of which I have already read. I don't know why I was so naïve to think it would get easier over time opening the box and reading the last words I will ever hear from my mother; it is anything but easy.

I sigh a defeated sigh and push myself up off the bed. I take the perfectly rectangular shaped box in my hands and sit on the edge of the bed cradling it, focusing on the meticulous detailed carvings that wrap around the entire wooden frame. I graze my fingers over the deep lines, tracing them, following their journey, anticipating where they will end. Surprisingly, they don't, they continue on, entwining together, enveloping and twisting in delicate symmetry, creating beautiful formations. I slide the lid back and lift out the letter titled: *Read on your Wedding Day.*

A wave of emotion washes through me as I hold my mother's letter in my hands. I don't know that I'm strong enough to read this. I wait patiently, hoping to be filled with some sort of courage, or have my worries suddenly all disappear like magic, making this whole ordeal laughable. *It's a letter from your parent's for you on your wedding day, my love, how bad could it be?* Roman's velvet voice croons in the back of my mind providing the comfort and the confidence needed to convince myself into opening the letter. I take in a sharp breath and I tear open the edge of the envelope. The letter reads:

Our dearest baby, Elle,

How time flies. It feels like only yesterday I found out I was pregnant with you and yet now you are getting married. Elle, it is important to us that you know how much love and happiness you have brought into our lives, and how very proud your dad and I are of the woman you have become. Neither your dad nor I can take the credit for the beauty within your soul or the kindness inside your heart. That is all you, honey.

Before you say "I do," we want you to take a breath and let it out slowly, releasing any and all worries, fears or concerns along with it. You will make such a wonderful wife, you will be exactly who your husband needs in every way.

It is our hope that you uplift each other and cherish one another's love equally. We pray that you understand the value of each other's hearts, and never take the exchange of your vows lightly. Above all else, always hold onto your love for each other and

remember the foundations in which it was built. Stand strong, united as one for always; you will need one another's love, honesty, and strength in this life.
We will be with you every step of the way, Ella. Forever and always.

Endless love,

Mom & Dad.

The words were more beautiful than I ever imagined they would be, though despite that, they cause everything within me to crumble. Hot tears spill down my cheeks, my heart is broken, shattered into a million pieces. If only I could pull the words off the page and create the image of my parents with them, just for one last hug, one last moment to tell them how much I love them.

A light breeze blows in through the window and when I turn, trembling, Roman is standing there, watching me. His presence is my undoing; I fall apart at the seams, but he catches me, his arms surrounding my body with his love, his warmth, my safe haven. He holds me against his chest, rocking me gently as my world falls to pieces and I lose myself in the grief I have tried so hard to suppress for so long.

As I lull in the comfort of my fiancé's arms, I'm ever grateful that he appeared when he did. Just like a dream.

"You broke tradition," I murmur quietly up at him as I turn to find his spectacular face.

"There was no way I couldn't, not after hearing the pain you were in. I had no other choice but to come to you." He peers down at me, brushing the hair out of my eyes. "I'll always come to you," he promised, pressing his lips to my forehead.

"I believe you," I reply.

Roman hugged me against his summer-warm body until I unwillingly fell into unconsciousness, sedated by his emanating heat.

When dawn broke, it glowed a beautifully soft orange-pink color that ignited the morning sky with immaculate radiance. I sat on the tire swing under the old oak tree and stared with amazement at the fabulously colored sky, idly wondering if Roman, too, was watching it at the same exact moment. What a captivating start to my wedding day, I thought, as the light Pacific breeze gently swayed the swing in its tame current.

The sound of Mr. Kahoa's truck rattling up the driveway caught my attention. Goodness, he was up early. I watched intently as he climbed out of the truck and made his way over to me. "Good morning, my dear," he said in *his* soft way.

"Good morning, Mr. Kahoa. What are you doing up so early this morning?"

He smiled, his cheeks scrunching into skinny smile-mounds. "I was on the early morning run to pick up the chairs from the youth center for the reception. Your dad had ordered a whole batch of new ones for the end of year performance last year, but because of what happened, the show was cancelled and the chairs were never used, so, I thought they would be perfectly utilized today," he smiled a little wider.

"You never let anything go to waste, do you, Mr. Kahoa?"

"No, not if I can help it, my dear."
I smiled, appreciating how similar Mr. Kahoa and Jack were.

I nod. "Just like my dad," I tighten my grip on the rope that secured myself and the swing to the creaking branch.

"Hmm," Mr. Kahoa murmured with a soft smile, then sat at my feet. "Ella, in honor of your father and the love he had for both you and my son, I would like to humbly offer myself as the man who walks beside you today and gives you away. I won't be hurt if you say no, but I—"
"I… I would actually really love that,"
"Well… I am really quite honored to hear you say that, my dear," he grinned widely, his eyes sparkling under the rising sun.
My emotions were beginning to get the better of me, and I was fighting against the

lump that was starting to form in my throat.

"Thank you, Mr. Kahoa." I managed to say.

"No, *thank you*, my darling. And, please, feel free to call me Dad, or Paul, which ever feels right to you. You are almost my daughter now too." His lips curled into that awkwardly shy Kahoa smile and I knew we were having a moment. "I will definitely consider it," I whispered a little too quietly, the realization that I had been unconsciously waiting for this moment dawned on me that it had finally arrived, and not a moment too soon. We smiled warmly at one another as Mr. Kahoa scaled to his feet and he leaned in, hugging me tightly for a brief few seconds.

"Hey, let me get in on some of that," Nova giggled as she bounced toward us holding a bottle of champagne and two flutes. She swung each of her arms around both her father and I and squeezed us together. "I love you guys," she sighed contently.

"Nova Rain, are you drunk?" Mr. Kahoa

asked sounding every bit amused. Nova frowned at her father, rolling her eyes.

"*Dad*, it's non-alcoholic." She muttered, sounding as if he should already know.

"Oh," he made a face, mocking his daughter. He mumbled something under his breath in Qaletaqa, sending Nova bouncing off toward his truck. When she returned, Nova held a small white box in her hands. She gave it to her father who then handed it to me. "Roman asked me to give this to you,"

I took the box and blinked blankly up at my soon-to-be father in-law.

"You saw Roman?" I asked.

Mr. Kahoa nodded, a soft smile touching his lips. "He was at the youth center this morning helping me load up the chairs into the back of the truck. He wanted you to have that." He shrugged his shoulders, his smile widening across his face once more.

Of course my Roman wakes before dawn to help load his father's truck with wedding supplies the morning of *his own wedding*. He is such a workaholic. I smile, then focus my attention on the box that sits in my hands. I lift off the lid and the newest iPhone is beaming back at me.

I smile, pressing the home button. The phone glowed to life with a photo of Roman as the lock screen wallpaper—he was blowing kisses.

"I don't know how you use those things," Mr. Kahoa chuckled as he poured champagne into each of the two glasses Nova was holding.

My new phone buzzed loudly. I quickly answered it.

"Hello?"

"Good morning my beautiful bride," Roman purred seductively.

His voice tightened every muscle below my waist in the most delicious way. I bit my lip in an attempt to stifle my smile.

"Good morning to you, too," I blushed.

"I see you received your gift." I could hear his smile through the phone.

"I did. You really didn't need to buy me anything,"

"Oh, but I did. You see, today I am

marrying the most beautiful creature I have ever laid eyes on, and I plan on giving her the world and all that comes with it… so, it is my duty to ensure she has every single thing that she could ever possibly want or need, and let's face it, you needed a new phone."

I giggle at his playfulness. I love hearing him sound like this.

"Indeed I did," I agree.

"Well, now that we have that out of the way and I have heard your voice, I will let you go so you can continue to get ready,"

I sigh. "Okay… I'll meet you at the altar." I whispered.

"I can't wait." He breathes, and I am all flushed imagining the smoldering brilliance in his eyes. *How can he make three little words hold so much promise?* I hang up and realize that Nova is staring at me with a contented expression, and handing me a half-full glass of champagne.

"What?" I accuse shyly.

Nova smiles widely and sings, "You lurrve him; you want to kiss him, hug him and marry him," and then clinks our glasses together. "Cheers," she beams brightly, then just as quickly becomes emotionally serious. "I wish you endless lifetimes together with undying happiness, passion, and love." We each sip at our non-alcoholic bubbles, the cool liquid running down my throat in the most soothing fashion. I smile, lost in thought, and Nova nudges my ribs, stealing my attention.

"You ready to get this party started?" she asks, her smile almost matching mine. I don't think about the answer, I just nod, a goofy smile floating on my lips.

"I'm *so* ready." I declare softly.

II

∞

I stare at my reflection in the floor-to-ceiling mirror as I smooth the palms of my hands over the French lace that is my wedding gown. *Wow,* I think to myself as a beautiful princess stares back at me. I'm lost for words at her beauty, at the happiness in her eyes. The woman in the mirror is a far cry from the ghost girl who used to look back at me all those months ago.

The bedroom door clicked closed behind me. I turn to greet my visitor but am frozen in place with unexpected shock from the emerald green eyes that catch mine upon meeting his gaze.

"Wow," he breathes, appearing stunned.

I smile nonchalantly, though his reaction touches something somewhere deep inside—somewhere I'm unwilling to explore.

"What are you doing here?" I demand, crossing my arms over my chest, almost protectively.

Kale's eyes stay fixed on mine for an extended moment but then fall to his now knotted fingers. "I-I just came from seeing Roman…" he stuttered nervously. "I don't want to cause any trouble, Elle."

"*Then why are you here?*"

Kale glances up at me, his eyes honest and wide.

"Honestly?" he asks.

I twist my mouth, unimpressed and impatient with his presence. He wouldn't want to be playing games, not today. He hesitates for a moment. He appears to be considering his answer. But right before my patience short-circuits and I order him out of the room, he runs his hand through his Johnny Depp slicked back hair and smiles that inherited Kahoa smile. "I want to be part of your big day," he raises his hands as he catches sight of the suspicious glare I am shooting him. "Before you say anything, no,

Roman wasn't happy about me just turning up the way I did but that's why I'm here... He told me to ask you for permission. He said whatever you say goes, so if you tell me to leave, I'll leave. But, Elle... I really want to be here to see my brother get married."

I eyed him suspiciously for as long as I could handle. His sincerity was evident in his words, his actions and in his eyes—there was simply no way of denying that. Of course I considered whether he was just a really good actor playing the part of the supportive brother... I mean, after what had transpired at Christmas, the way he forced himself on me, the evil-promising look in his eyes, how he said it wasn't over... I shook my head to rid myself of the negative memories.

"You want to be here to watch your brother get married..." I spoke with slow precision as I repeated his words. Kale nodded cautiously. "Even though he's marrying *me*?"

"Especially because he is marrying you," he blurted out, seemingly without thinking.

"What does *that* mean?"

"I-I-I don't know," he let out a deep

gush of air as he exhaled, dropping his face into his hands. "I've had a lot of time to think about everything and I am honestly so disgusted with myself for how I've treated you, Elle. Look, it's no secret how I feel about you, but I'm trying to turn over a new leaf and make positive decisions and changes."

I drop onto the edge of the bed, keeping a good distance between us. "Why?" I ask speculatively. Kale's eyes soften and he takes one step toward me. My hand automatically flies up in response, warning him to stop. Kale backs himself into the door behind him, his eyes apologetic.

"I want to be in your life, Elle. Even if that means I have to stand back and watch you live your life with my brother. I-I love you enough to let you go, I just, I need to be in your life," his eyes burn with intense emotion as he watches me try and figure out how I feel about all this. I'm thrown, even despite already being fully aware of his feelings for me, but more so because I wasn't expecting any of this, especially not today. I let my head fall back limply and I glare up at the ceiling, willing the tornado of emotions inside me to calm like the eye of a storm. I release a defeated sigh, shifting my gaze back to Kale who is still frozen by the door, gaping at me expectantly.

"You can stay," I say, my voice small. "But. You keep away from me. Do you understand?"

His brilliant smile slips, fading from his full lips. He nods once. "As you wish." Sadness clouds his features as he half bows, turning on his heel, leaving the room, and closing the door behind him.

I hug myself, taking in a deep breath and releasing it. Lena's instructions from the wedding day letter prominent in my mind. *Breathe and release slowly.*

The door creaks open again and Mr. Kahoa pops his head around the corner.

"Are you alright, my dear?" he smiles and in that moment he looks so much like an older version of Roman. I can't hide my smile. I nod offering reassurance, though I am unsure of why he is asking. Is it because of Kale's unexpected arrival? Or perhaps because it was my wedding day and two of the most important people in my life aren't here. Whatever the reason, I find myself a lot more at ease now that he is here with me.

"I'm fine," I say, standing, straightening

the sheath lace of my gown.

Mr. Kahoa returns my smile as he walks toward me, taking my hands in his, a look of awe on his face.

"You are absolutely breathtaking," he inhales sharply. "I wish your parents could see you right now. How proud they would be," we smile goofily at one another, and I try my hardest to fight back the tears that are harrowingly close to rolling down my freshly powdered cheeks.

Mr. Kahoa kisses my left hand. "My son is the luckiest man I know." He murmurs over the lump that is audibly forming in his throat.

I wrap my arms around my soon to be father in-law's shoulders, hugging him tightly.

"Thank you," I breathe. "Not just for saying all that, but for being here for me today and standing in for my dad, and mostly for making such a wonderful man for me to marry. You and Dena have given me the greatest gift I could have ever asked for."

He pulls away then, tears in his eyes.

"No, my dear, you have that the wrong way around," he says with a gentle smile imprinting his lips. "Your parents gave us the greatest gift by giving us you. You have breathed new life into our home, our son, and our lives. It is an honor to have you become an official member of our family today, Ella."

His words are my undoing. Hot beads of tears roll down my face as Mr. Kahoa envelopes me in his arms once more. The door opens once more, but this time Nova and Dena shuffle in.

"Dad! You made her cry? Ugh, now I have to fix her makeup." Nova barks at her father, making us both giggle as we wipe away our tears.

"What?" he shrugs his broad shoulders. "They're happy tears." He replied in defense. Nova rolled her eyes.

"You still look stunning, darling." Dena adds as she softly weeps into a tissue.

"Thank you," I begin to thank her but Nova snatches my hand and drags me over to the antique vanity table in the corner of the room, shoving me onto the white leather ottoman in front of the mirror.

"No. No thank you. We have to fix your makeup. Now." She panics as her hands fumble nervously over the makeup brushes and the endless array of pressed powders.

"She's right, my dear, it's almost time to go." Mr. Kahoa agrees, checking his watch.

I gape at my soon to be father in-law in the mirror. Shock and nervousness are beginning to settle in.

"How long?" I ask softly, barely able to hear my own question.

"Ten minutes, darling." Dena advised in her calm tone before becoming a blubbery mess all over again.

Nova smiles, rolling her eyes heavenward as she finishes the final touches on my makeup.

"No more crying," She warns, grinning from ear-to-ear. "Or I'll have to hurt you."

"Okay." I mouth.

Ten minutes? I stress, wondering where all the time has gone. I could have sworn there was still half an hour left at the very least. I breathe; in through the nose, out through the mouth. *Why am I so nervous?* I stare at my reflection as I ask myself this question. I look beautiful. Exactly how I envisioned myself on my wedding day. And I am marrying the man of my dreams— literally. I had nothing to be nervous about, and yet, I couldn't shake this strange feeling that kept popping up and attacking every fiber in my body. I forced myself to redirect my thinking.

"How does it look out there?" I ask. The question was for no one in particular, I just needed it answered to give me something positive to think about.

"Oh, Elle. You are going to fall in love. You really have an eye for detail. All your ideas have come together beautifully." Dena says, relieving my concerns, forcing my mind to fill with happier thoughts.

"I told everyone you were a natural at wedding planning back when you helped me with mine." Nova teased, reminding me of a time not so long ago that being given this exact compliment almost made me cringe, and yet today, it provoked positive emotions.

"It's time." Mr. Kahoa announces, opening the door.

My heart skips a beat right in that moment—the nervousness threatening to flood my system once more. But then I think about Roman waiting for me at the altar. I imagine how amazingly handsome he must look, and then that was it—I couldn't contain my excitement to see him from that moment on.

III

As we descended the stairs, Nova was having a hard time containing her excitement.

"I can't wait for you to see everything. The garden looks stunning. And the barn is something straight out of a fairytale." She squeals, elated, as she glides ahead of me in her shimmery blush tulle tea length dress with her ebony hair set in a soft crown on top of her head.

I let out a deep breath as we approach the doors. My hand nervously clasped tightly around Mr. Kahoa's arm.

"Deep breaths, my dear." He whispers as we follow Nova into the garden.

I concentrate extra hard on my breathing, counting each breath in and out of my lungs, and watch my feet with every step closer I take toward Roman. I am too afraid to look up at the decorations or the people who stand patiently awaiting my arrival. I'm afraid if I look up and see everyone staring back at me that it will send me over the edge into a full-blown anxiety attack.

"Here we go, love." The familiar tone of my dad's voice floats beside me and when my neck snaps up to look at Mr. Kahoa, I see Jack standing beside me, grinning like the proudest father in the world. I blink again and Mr. Kahoa's russet face smiles back at me.

My feet touch the beginning of the lace trimmed burlap runner which has white rose petals scattered all down the center of the aisle, and as Mr. Kahoa guides me forward, I finally lift my eyes to find Roman.

There he was, standing under a wooden arch overflowing with white orchids and roses, staring back at me; his eyes smiling, his perfect face exuding the depth of his emotion and love for me. He was all I saw as Mr. Kahoa and I continued down the aisle, and as our eyes met, his lips broke into his breathtaking Kahoa smile, a smile of reveling satisfaction.

That urgency I'd been experiencing so frequently flooded every muscle and I struggled to pace my steps to the rhythm of the soft music that surrounded us, quickening my steps forward, wanting to reach Roman more than anything else I had desired as of late. But finally, I reached the end of the lace trimmed burlap aisle. Roman held out his hand, intently waiting. And in a tradition as old as time, Mr. Kahoa kissed my cheek, and placed my hand in Roman's. The magical warmness of his lips touched the back of my hand and I was home.

Whilst we wrote our own vows, Roman was adamant about including the traditional words as well. And in the exact moment that the officiant pronounced us husband and wife, my whole world, which had been ripped apart and turned upside down for so long now, seemed to calm and settle; showing me that all my worries and fears about getting married were beyond pointless.

"You may now kiss your beautiful

bride." The officiant announced, and Roman pulled me into him, holding me ever so gently, and as his lips hovered above mine, I looked into his tear-filled, triumphant gaze and I realized I had won, too. And as our lips met I knew nothing else mattered except for us.

Our audience burst into a loud roar behind us as they clapped and cheered gleefully. I tried to comprehend, through the wave of emotion saturating every crack and scar of my soul, the unimaginable reality that this beautiful man was now mine forever. Roman pulled away from our kiss just enough to glance into my eyes, his lips quirking up into *his smile*, his eyes burning such a deep profound joy, and I felt our souls imprint and bind together, eternally linking us for the rest of time.

"Wow," I managed to choke out in an almost unintelligible whisper.

"Wow indeed, Mrs. Kahoa." Roman leaned in, kissing me tenderly, adoringly, feeling what I felt just as deeply—if not more.

It was Nova and Dena who reached us first,

enfolding us into their scorching embraces, their tear-streaked faces the first thing we saw when we unwillingly tore our eyes away from each other. And then I was passed from person to person, warm embrace to warm embrace as my new family members congratulated me and lovingly welcomed me into the family. But the absence of the two people I needed there the most was so significant that at times I felt I was trying exceptionally hard to portray the 'blushing bride' more than I could handle. Though, whenever I would become upset I would get a sudden whiff of Jack's musky cologne or I would hear Lena's laugh, and I knew they were here with us, with me.

The orange sun set behind the trees and the celebrations at the ceremony continued on into the reception.

The old barn that Roman had once so romantically decorated was now the epitome of every dream I ever held when I thought about my wedding day. White rose petals were scattered over the entire floor, white drapery hung from beam to beam with strands of soft white lights wrapping around and down every wooden beam and pillar, the tables were so delicately decorated with fine linen and white orchid centerpieces atop rustic tree slabs. And keeping to the theme, all of the timeless traditions were kept; hundreds of photos, cutting of the cake, throwing of my bouquet, and then there was our first dance as husband and wife.

Roman twirled me onto the dancefloor, catching me expertly as the soft music began to play, and we swayed effortlessly under the twinkling veil of lights.

"Enjoying yourself, Mrs. Kahoa?" he whispered into my ear.

I smiled. "Indeed I am, Mr. Kahoa."

Roman's eyes softened. "I know this is hard without them," he murmured, pressing his lips to my cheek. "But I know they are here with us," he smiled widely. "Not even death could keep Jack and Lena from attending your wedding."

"*Our* wedding." I corrected.

"Our wedding." Roman agreed, leaning down to kiss me softly as we danced arm in arm.

The music changed and Mr. Kahoa claimed the father-daughter dance. He was just as skilled at slow dancing as his son was, so it made it all-the-more-easier for me and my two left feet.

"Your parents would be so proud of you." He said, his lined face smiling.

I nodded in agreeance. "I sense them here, you know." I confessed, placing my cheek on my father-in-law's shoulder. I felt him chuckle silently before he kissed the top of my head. "I have no doubt, my dear. I feel them here, too." He held me a little tighter then and we stayed like that until the song played its last note.

Roman left me to dance with almost every guest at the party while he tended to some "important business." When I finally had time to take a break and sit for a few seconds, Kale made his way over.

"May I have this dance?" he asked, holding out his hand.

I glared at him speculatively, but since he had kept his word and stayed away from me all evening, I felt I owed him at least one dance.

It wasn't as comfortable being this close to Kale as it had been with everyone else tonight. It had nothing to do with his dancing, because he was a Kahoa after all and it seemed an inherited trait that they could all dance spectacularly well, whatever the reason, I couldn't put my finger on it, so I tried not to dwell on it for too long.

"Thank you," he breathed.

"For what?"

"For allowing me this opportunity to show you—and my brother—that I am trying to change."

"I think I see that." I admitted.

"Yeah?" he sounded almost shocked by my answer.

I nodded, pulling back to find his eyes. "I do." I smiled.

Suddenly his face dropped as if in pain and he left me standing in the middle of the dancefloor alone and utterly confused.

It wasn't long before Roman was back and we were dancing our last dance of the night.

"Do you have any idea how heartbreakingly beautiful you are?"

"Stop it. I am just as I am every other day except with this grand gown and curled hair."

Roman's smile was amused, almost a smirk. "My point still stands." He whispered, his lips inches from my own.

"You are an impossible husband." I declare, gazing into Roman's tawny eyes.

"And, you, an impossible wife. I suppose we were made for each other." His lips curl once more before he kisses me, ignoring our audience.

Before the night came to an end, Nova and Manti presented us with our wedding gift. It was wrapped in the most beautiful paper, making me hesitate to rip it open, but Roman insisted. I held a familiar deep mahogany wooden box in my hands and when I opened it, my eyes welled with an uncontrollable flood of tears and I was rendered speechless.

"We thought having something from your parents on your wedding day was the best gift we could give you." Nova spoke softly.

"But, this-this is yours. They gave this flute to you and Manti for your engagement."

"Ella, we want you and Roman to have it. It is our gift to you." Nova and Manti both smiled humbly as I wrapped my arms around them and hugged them tightly.

"Thank you." I whispered.

"Speaking of gifts. Mrs. Kahoa, will you come with me please?" Roman took the wooden flute box in one hand and my hand in the other and led me out into the swath of the night.

"Where are you taking me?" I asked, unable to see a thing through the heavy darkness.

"You'll see."

"That's it? That's all I get?" I complain, playfully. Roman ignored me, and continued tugging me toward something in the distance. I could swear I almost saw an imprint of a soft smile but I couldn't be sure due to the lack of light.

I hear the sound of crashing waves and I know we are on the cliff. Roman stops us before reaching the center of the overhanging rock and stands in front of me as if to shield me from seeing something.

"What I'm about to show you will give you the answers to a lot of the questions I know you have." His warm hands cradle my face ever so gently, and he kisses me sweetly before stepping aside, allowing me to look beyond the cliff at something that held the answers I apparently craved.

IV

∞

The waves carried hundreds of flickering orange lights, gracefully floating along the ripples of the dark sea, until finally coming to their final resting place on the shore.

My heart raced as flashbacks to the night of my twenty-first birthday swamped my mind. Either this was a seriously impeccable case of déjà vu or all the answers adding up in my head were true.

I turned and faced Roman who was already looking at me. I wanted to cry and laugh and scream all at the same time, but all I could do was look into the loving eyes of my husband and say the only thing I knew was true.

"It was you," I forced over the lump in my throat.

Roman nodded, a soft smile touching his lips.

"This whole time… it was… you?"

"Yes."

"And at the bar?" I asked.

"Yes."

"And… and in the car lot at the diner that night?" I held my breath.

Roman nodded. "Yes, then too."

I exhaled and ran my hands through my hair. I was in shock, or disbelief, or I was grateful. I couldn't make sense of my feelings.

"I… I don't know what to say, Roman."

"That's okay," he reassured me. "I just wanted you to know it—"

"Why didn't you tell me back then? Why didn't you just show yourself to me?" I hadn't intended to cut him off and lose my temper but I couldn't exactly control it either. I felt his hands move to the nape of my neck and his lips brushed against my hair.

"I'm sorry. I was trying to keep my distance from you back then, trying to protect you. But staying away from you was harder than I expected it to be. I wanted to be so close to you on your birthday. I wanted to kiss you and hold you more than I'd wanted anything in my life. But I didn't want to drag you into this dangerous and miserable life."

His words quelled my angry thoughts and feelings and I wrapped my arms around his waist, looking up at him.

"It's not miserable. I'm not miserable, Roman. I am the happiest I have ever been."

"I know you are," his smile touched his eyes then and he caressed my cheek with his warm thumb. "That's why I thought it only right that I tell you the truth."

"Hmm…"

"What?"

"Oh, nothing. It was your loss," I teased. "You see, the dark knight who saved me in the car lot probably would have been rewarded with a kiss for his heroic efforts. But, since you didn't tell me it was you…"

"Oh, really?" Roman challenged.

"Really indeed."

"But I can kiss you anytime I want."

"This is true, but *that kiss* would have been a special kiss. It would have been the start of something magical."

"Ella, the first moment I saw you was the start of something magical. Every kiss since then has only added to the spellbinding power you have over me—don't you know that?"

Snap. He got me. I became lost in the marvelous way he watched me and in the tender way he held me, willing my forgiveness for keeping this secret for so long.

We looked out over the edge of the cliff until all the flames went out and then Roman played the most captivating music on the flute, again, keeping to tradition.

Before the sun rose, Roman insisted on one more surprise. We walked along the border of the Kahoa's land and into the dense and dark trees that lined the edge of their property. Roman covered my eyes for the full effect, as he so humorously put it, and when we finally came to a halt, he lifted his hands away and I opened my eyes.

A cozy stone and timber log cabin stood before us. It was single story but the grandest thing I had ever seen. I wondered idly how I had never noticed it before.

"Wow, Roman, it's beautiful."

"I'm glad you like it." He handed me a set of keys.

I stared blankly at the silver keys as he placed them in my palm.

"The house is yours." He whispered with a satisfied smirk on his face.

I blinked wildly up at him.

"You bought it for me?" I asked, stunned.

He shook his head. "No," he breathed against my lips. "I built it for you."

I gasped, utterly floored.

"Roman…" I couldn't find the words.

"I told you I would give you the world and everything in it," I heard his smile as I stared in awe at my new home. "Would you like to see inside?"

I nodded, still without the ability to speak.

The interior of our home was just as breathtaking as the exterior. And when we finally found our bedroom, I knew, tonight was the perfect moment Roman had been waiting for.

"Roman, I—" he placed his finger over

my lips.

"Shh." He shook his head, his eyes blazing fervently. He laced my neck with seductive kisses as we moved to our bed.

Bursts of fire exploded into the early morning night sky, illuminating our room with the most spectacular colors. And we made love.

At last.

The glow from the crackling fire still ignited our room in the most sensual shade of orange I had ever seen, or perhaps I was delusional, still spellbound by the way Roman made love to me. Twice.

I felt Roman stir, tightening his arms around my shoulders, gently, careful not to hurt me. He looked down at me, waiting for my eyes to meet his before his pressed his lips to mine.

"Good morning," he purred.

"Hmm," I murmured, finding his lips once more. "I thought we already said that." I teased, reminding him of our very salacious early-morning wake-up call.

"We did," he smiled, tangling our fingers between the spaces of our hands. "But we were… preoccupied. And besides, I can't have my beautiful bride thinking I don't know how to greet her."

I stifled my laugh, opting for a more flirtatious expression. "Judging by the two times you 'greeted' me this morning, I highly doubt I will have any objections to how you greet me in the future."

Roman kissed my temple, chuckling silently.

"Speaking of our future, we should get up and start heading to the airport."

"Already?" I turn in his arms to face him.

"Yes," he nods. "I want to escape with you before anyone else has a chance to steal you away from me. Nova especially," he pulls a face, rolling his eyes, then smiles down at me. "As of the moment we walked away from our wedding, I have wanted nothing more than to whisk you away and have you all to myself."

I giggle, holding up my left hand. "You get to keep me forever, remember, Mr. Kahoa?"

"Forever will never be long enough, Mrs. Kahoa." His dark eyes watch me intently.

"I love you," I say.

"More, baby." He replies.

I groan inwardly. Time to get up and head to the airport.

"Hawaii, here we come!" I announce, sitting up in bed, preparing to make my way to the bathroom.

I wrap the white cotton sheet around my naked body, giving Roman a quick lascivious grin, when suddenly he tugs the sheet as I stand, pulling me back to the bed, crashing into his bare chest.

"Actually," he says. "I thought our honeymoon could be up in the Alaskan mountains,"

"No Hawaii?" I pout.

"I know you had your heart set on Hawaii, but the old man chief has a cabin up in the mountains that I really want to take you to. It's a little more rustic than the five-star resort you wanted, but—"

"Wait. How rustic are we talking here?"

"No hot water or electricity." His lips quirk up into an apologetic smile.

"That's not rustic—that is primitive!"

Roman's smile widens. "I know, I know, but we can go hiking in the mountains and there are hot springs all over the place. We can go swimming just like you wanted," he pauses, waiting for my answer. "I promise it won't be as horrific as you are imagining."

I make a face. This is not what I envisioned my honeymoon to be like.

"You're not keen are you?"

I roll my eyes and wrap my arms around Roman's neck.

"No, I am… I honestly don't care where we are, as long as I'm with you."

"Really?"

"Yes really." I smile.

Roman's face lights up as he leans into me, his lips caressing mine.

∞

After a quick layover in Seattle, we finally board our last flight. This plane is small and rickety as it taxis down the runway. Roman triple-checks my seatbelt, again, tugging and shaking it to ensure its safety. I'm starting to think he is a nervous flyer.

"Not nervous," he mumbled under his breath. "Just cautious." He winks, tucking a loose tendril of hair back behind my ear, kissing my lips chastely before sitting in his seat and fastening his own belt.

"Uhuh." I grin back at him.

As the plane begins to lift off the ground I nestle into Roman's chest. He envelopes his arms around my body, holding me against him as securely as he can manage.

"I'm safe," I murmur into his ear.

His eyes find mine and a slightly nervous smile imprints his lips

"I love you." I whisper, hoping it will ease his anxiety.

Roman's hold tightens protectively and we stay like that for the next three hours.

After having collected our luggage we wait outside by the sculptures that line the sidewalk in front of the airport. A shiny black Audi pulls up beside us and comes to a halt. A small man with black hair introduces himself as Eli, congratulates us on our marriage, and takes our luggage, putting it into the trunk.

Roman can't take his eyes off me the whole ride to the cabin. His stare is full of love, yet dark and alluring, and with a slight curl of his lips, every muscle south of my navel tenses in the most delicious way, sending a rush of butterflies flooding my entire being.

I sink my teeth into my lower lip, and I watch him, my heart racing.

The car slows and turns down a long and secluded driveway. At the very end is a small provincial cabin, surrounded by woodlands, with smoke billowing out of the chimney.

Roman raises his brows, a coy smile touching his lips as he opens the car door and steps out into the brisk air. I follow.

"Thank you for the ride, Eli." Roman hands our driver some money, then turns his attention back to me.

He leans in, his lips hovering inches from my ear, and every part of my body blushes.

"I feel it too," Roman's teeth tug and nibble at my earlobe, I moan and I'm undone. Aching for his touch, his kiss, all of him, I fall into his embrace. Roman's mouth claims my neck; his tongue gliding along my skin as he laces my neck in seductive kisses, his hands gently tangling in the waves of my hair. I close my eyes, savoring the sensation.

Roman swiftly lifts me into his arms and carries me inside. Our eyes are locked on each other, our bodies crooning the same love song.

"I want you." He breathes.

"I want you too." I reply, all breathy.

"You're mine," he says against my lips.

"All yours." I promise as he lays me onto the bed.

"Every. Single. Part. Of you." He declares between each tear of my clothing.

Each word is more enticing than the last. Roman rips off his shirt and tosses our shredded clothing to the floor. His smoldering eyes watch me greedily as he lowers his naked body to mine with infinite slowness. The anticipation is so electrifying that my breathing picks up and I am almost panting fervently with want.

"Turn over." Roman says, flipping me deftly.

"You're so beautiful." He says in a low tone as he lowers his mouth to the nape of my neck.

His tongue slowly runs along my spine, sending tantalizing tingles throughout my body. He stops as he reaches my behind.

"Spread your legs." He says, his hands softly running over my backside and along the top of my thighs.

I do as I'm asked and open my legs a few inches apart.

"That's good. That's enough. Now, be still."

Roman trails his tongue along the center of my behind until he reaches my sex.

"Oh!"

"Shh, baby." He growls, flipping me onto my back.

This time, Roman bites and licks at my neck, then drags his tongue along the center of my breasts, down my stomach, all the way down until he reaches the apex of my thighs once more.

"Roman," I beg, but he doesn't listen.

I feel his smile as his tongue touches me, and I surrender to my husband and all his gratifying torture.

I tangle my fingers in his long silky hair as he works his magic, bringing me close to the brink of euphoria, but he stops, quickly moving up my body, his lips finding mine.

Our tongues dance in unison as we kiss passionately. Roman lowers himself against me, and slowly, gently, sinks inside me.

V

The next week played out pretty much the same way. We never really left the room unless absolutely necessary. Roman would cook using the wood oven and that alone would take anywhere from three to four hours, giving us plenty of time to focus on each other.

I had no idea Roman was such an expert cook. We ate tender roasts and stews from freshly hunted deer the locals would gift us, and at night we roasted marshmallows by candlelight. Roman made certain our honeymoon was just as magical as our wedding ceremony, leaving no leaf unturned. I felt like the luckiest woman in the entire existence of the world.

The last week of our tranquil holiday had finally rolled around and as much as I had enjoyed staying closed away indoors, under the covers with my husband, I found myself wanting to explore the mountains and experience a little bit of what Alaska had to offer.

"Do you remember the way you sold this honeymoon to me?" I asked, fighting back the sarcasm in my tone.

Roman pulled the quilt over us, wrapping his arms around my waist and dragging me across the bed and into his fiery warm chest.

"Sold it? I don't recall *selling* it to you," he grinned mischievously as he nuzzled my neck.

"You lie!" I laugh. "You promised adventure and hiking, and—and hot springs." I give my best pouty face.

Roman smiles my favorite smile, melting the core of my soul; I know without a doubt that if I wasn't so adamant about experiencing the hot springs, I would surely be lead astray by his seductive expression.

"Ah, so it is adventure my wife wants."

I nod. "You promised."

"That I did," he finally admits. "But, you know, I would just as happily stay right here with you for the next week." He whispered, his lips claiming mine.

"I'm not changing my mind," I say softly, before I tear myself away and out of the bed.

Reluctantly, Roman leaves our bed. He finds me in the kitchen where I am boiling some hot water on the fire.

"Leave that," he murmurs against my ear as he comes up behind me. "I'll draw you a bath when we get back."

I turn in his arms, smiling as I look up at him. "We're going?" I ask and he smiles softly down at me as he wraps a loose tendril of hair behind my ear.

"Of course we're going."

The hot spring was nothing at all what I expected it to be. It was better. I expected man-made pools filled to the brink with people. Whilst there is a resort that offers such a thing, Roman and I hiked up a secluded densely covered mountain trail that opened up onto a cliff overlooking a grand cliff-edge backdrop, bejeweled with lush green forest and exposed rock. A natural mineral hot spring sunk into the edge of the cliff, surrounded by fallen tree logs and large stones. A waterfall trickled into the spring from the above river that swept through the forest, giving the atmosphere a serene and soothing feel. And as the day turned to night, the northern lights came alive in the night sky, bathing us in a magical green glow.

"This is the most breathtaking thing I have ever seen," I sigh, looking up at the colorful sky.

"It is beautiful," Roman agrees, gliding his hand up and down my back. "But nowhere near as beautiful as you." He declares, his voice full of dark and sensual desire.

I can't help but smile.

"You're biased." I say, turning to face him.

"I'm allowed to be." He growls, wrapping my legs around his waist and kissing me fervidly. Every muscle south of my body tenses in a delicious fashion as salacious desire unfurls deep inside me.

Roman's fingers fiddle with the string of my bikini and with one quick tug, I am bare chested. Roman's eyes watch me, carefully, intently, taking in every inch of my naked body. His tongue sweeps across his bottom lip as he stares hungrily. I feel his arousal growing beneath me as he wraps my hair around his hand and gently tugs my head to the side, my neck exposed and at his mercy as he trails feather-light kisses up to my ear.

"You. Are. So. Beautiful." He breathes, sending an array of tingles through me.

His words, his touch, his soft carnal kisses are driving me wild. I fear if he doesn't take me now I'm going to combust.

Roman hears my desirous plea. Never taking his eyes off mine, he tears off my bikini bottoms, lifts me effortlessly in the water and pushes himself into me. His eyes blaze lasciviously and all the air escapes my lungs.

I moan with pleasure, grinding my hips, matching his rhythm. I'm undone and at his mercy. My mind swims as I climax.

"Roman," I cry, and I catch a glimpse of his triumphant smile as I throw my head back. Roman's hands touch me greedily, then he wraps his hand around the nape of my neck and pulls me into him, his tongue invading my mouth.

"Open your eyes. I want to see you." He murmurs as he bites into my bottom lip.

I do as I'm told, wanting more than anything to please my husband. We watch each other as we make love.

"I love you," he says, his voice hoarse, his breathing harsh.

Before I can say anything he slams into me—hard—and we both groan as he hits my sweet spot and pours himself into me, my breath hitches in my throat, Roman growls, and his temperature soars to an all-time high. I collapse against his chest, burrowing my face into his neck, I inhale his scent.

I don't have the energy to move. We are warm, in each other's arms and our sexual appetite is satisfied—for now.

The loud banging of the wooden shutters hitting the cabin wakes me. I am momentarily disorientated. It's dark outside and the wind is howling and whistling as it's gale force currents beat against the old timber house.

I smell the delicious scent of bacon wafting through the room. With my stomach taking the lead, I wrap myself in the heavy quilt from the end of the bed and make my way out to the kitchen. I find Roman—in only his sweat pants—cooking breakfast on the fire.

"Good morning," he murmurs, handing me a cup of hot chocolate.

"Morning," I smile, feeling suddenly shy after our little hot spring rendezvous last night. "You're cooking." I point at the skillet of bacon.

"Yeah, I thought you might be hungry after our swim last night." He smiles warmly, though his eyes are dancing with dark amusement.

"Mmhmm." I take a sip of my hot chocolate to stifle my grin and sit by the fire in the main room.

Before too long, Roman joins me, placing the hot skillet on the stone fireplace, and I lean against his chest, seldom needing the fire to keep me warm.

The wind picks up, sounding even more violent than before. I shudder, cold shivers wracking my body. Roman curls his arms around me, holding me close.

"There's a storm coming. I should go hunting before visibility gets too low."

"You are not going out in *that*." I scoff. I feel Roman chuckle silently against my back.

"We need food. This was the last of our supply." He says, handing me the last strip of crunchy bacon.

"Ok, but what animal is going to be out in this?" I point toward the window.

"I'll find something. I've already drawn a bath for you, it should be the perfect temperature by now. Come on." Roman stands, picking me up and carrying me into the bathroom.

The cedar bath is filled almost to the brink with hot water. The steam smells of jasmine and cherry blossoms. I inhale deeply and exhale slowly as Roman begins to undress me.

"I can do that," I say gingerly. "You should start your hunt."

"Okay. Any requests?"

"Only that you come home in one piece."

"I can do that." He smiles, tilting my head back and pressing his lips to mine.

"I love you." I remind him.

"More, baby."

As I soak in the hot tub, I close my eyes and allow myself to drift back to the last few weeks we have spent here. I relish the quality time we have spent together, the conversations we have had about our future and all the things we have to look forward to. I feel as though I really lucked out when destiny worked its magic and brought Roman and I together. He is most definitely everything I have ever dreamed of. I delight in the fact that we have overcome every hurdle that popped up along the way. We are strong people individually, but so much stronger together.

All I can think of as our time in Alaska comes to an end, is how excited I am to begin our life together as husband and wife, Chief and Chieftess of the Qaletaqa wolf pack, and king and queen of our new home. All our troubles seem like such a distant memory, and for that, I am glad.

A loud thud steals my attention, pulling me from my reverie. I clamber out of the tub, drying myself as fast as I can manage and race to the room to dress before I get too cold. As I enter the room I notice the white mist outside the window. *Oh no.* It is snowing and Roman still isn't back.

I throw on Roman's snow jacket and I head outside. There is absolutely zero visibility. I can barely see my own hand in front of my face. I can't believe my husband is out there in this weather.

As I begin to fear the worst and panic starts to set in, I suddenly catch a glimpse of a dark figure in the distance. Every fiber in my body urges me forward in the hopes it is Roman returning home safe and sound, but something in the back of my mind stops me dead in my tracks. I can only put it off to the fact I am standing alone in the Alaskan mountains during one of the most severe snow storms ever to hit the state; I pause and then I hear the gruff grunt of what sounds like a bear.

Slowly and cautiously, I back myself into the cabin, closing the door as quietly as I can manage with trembling hands. I lock the door, vaguely wondering whether it would do any good if the bear decides to bust through the old timber door, and I keep watch by the bedroom window. As I watch the bear make his way up to the front door, I pray Roman doesn't come home whilst the bear is searching for food. It scratches and pounds viciously at the door, and by the grace of God the door withstands the beating, staying in tact and closed.

After what feels like hours, the bear disappears in the misty haze of snow, leaving me to fret over Roman's safety and whereabouts.

As nightfall encroaches, I feed some more wood into the fire, watching as it flares up, sparking and crackling wildly, and I wait for Roman to arrive home. I curl up on the old chesterfield sofa and reluctantly drift off to sleep.

I am startled awake by the howl of a wolf in the near distance. My heart races as I scramble off the sofa, dashing out the front door with no concern for my own safety. It is dark and the snow is still falling, almost in sheets.

Roman catches me just as I leap out the door, wrapping me in his arms and burying his face in my hair.

"Ella, I'm okay. I'm here. I'm home." He says as he breathes me in.

I squeeze him as tight as I can manage, not willing to let him go.

"I was so worried about you,"

"I know. I'm sorry." He says, taking my face in his hands.

"Don't ever leave me alone like that again." I implore, staring into Roman's eyes. He wipes away a tear I hadn't realized was escaping down my cheek.

"I won't ever leave you again," he presses his lips to mine, sealing his promise in a kiss.

Once inside, I lead Roman to the fire and undress him. I am surprised to find his clothes are only lightly damp, and as I drape them over the sofa, I realize his body temperature was the underlying reason. *Ah, the perks of being a wolf.* I smile at the thought and find my way back into my husband's warm embrace. We lay entwined together by the fire, and I listen intently as he tells me of his journey. He had come across the bear whilst out hunting by the river. They almost came to blows over some salmon, but Roman was able to frighten the bear away. On his way home, Roman had caught the bear's scent and followed it right back to the cabin. He told me how proud he was of me for holding down the fort and for being brave. I decided not to tell him how scared I really was, you know, not wanting to ruin the moment.

Roman held me tightly, protectively

against his side, only getting up once he heard my stomach growl in hunger, pulling some salmon from a small cooler.

"Oh, thank God, I'm starving!" I sighed in relief.

"You and me both," Roman's eyes glowed seductively. Closing the cooler, he leans into me, lacing my neck in slow, sensual kisses.

"I was talking about dinner," I say softly, enjoying every second his tongue touches my skin.

I feel Roman smile against my neck.

"Is that all I'm good for? Hunting and bringing back dinner?" he feigns hurt feelings, forcing my smile.

"No… not *only* that." I tease.

"Good, coz I was talking about how ravenous I am for you."

"Oh? Really? Ravenous?" I flutter my lashes up at him.

"Indeed, Mrs. Kahoa." He growls, all breathy and sexy as hell, taking me then and there by the fireplace.

VI

∞

Back to reality and in Featherbrook, Roman and I emanated an amazing post-wedding glow that everyone commented on. We were practically inseparable.

On Friday evening, Roman had finished work early and we had planned to go for a walk along the beach, but before we left I received a call from the post office saying they had an undelivered parcel for me and that I had to pick it up or they would return it to the sender by the end of that business day. It was a minor detour, nothing Roman was too fussed about. We decided to take Sapphire since the weather was nice, the breeze abnormally warm, and we opened the sunroof as we cruised along the scenic route into town.

Roman smiled as he curled his arm around my waist, dragging me across the seat into his body.

Everything seemed to be in slow motion for some reason… I stared at my husband, lost in his beauty, fighting the anxiety that was undeniably building within my veins for no apparent reason. It almost felt like an out of body experience; I was there, but I was watching us from the other side of the car.

Roman's husky laugh captures my attention.

"I love you," he whispers. A sudden urgency I am all too familiar with washes through me; an urgency to capture his words, his smile, this moment… and then it happened. We are horrifically blindsided with a mighty crack! My neck snaps in one direction and I fly out of Roman's arms. Everything is spinning. The wheels are screaming as if in unimaginable pain, and my body smashes against something hard, then I am thrown through the windshield, into mid-air, until I land on the ground with a loud slap. Everything turns black.

When I wake, my head feels heavy. I try lifting it but the weight of the pounding is too severe. I give up, opting to lay on my stomach with my face pressed to the cold, wet gravel.

I survey my surroundings from where I lay, though my vision is impaired somewhat. I try to focus on my breathing, and I eventually find the strength to lift my hands to rub my eyes. I see what looks like my car. It is down an embankment, laying on its roof. The tires are still spinning at a snail like pace. *Roman?* I cry in my mind. All at once, I panic as the realization of what has just happened dawns on me.

A small burst of adrenaline shoots through my body and I push myself up off the road, trying to find my footing. A wave of dizziness overcomes me and I fall. Out of fear of Roman being injured I try again, this time steadying myself against a nearby tree. Losing my balance, I stumble down the hill until I hit what is left of Sapphire.

I scramble to my feet, pulling at every door-handle, hoping the next one won't be so busted up that I can get inside to help Roman. He is hanging upside down, unconscious.

"Roman!" I scream. "Baby! Roman, wake up!" I bang furiously against the glass.

Seeing no other option, I crawl back through the shattered windscreen. I check for his pulse but can find nothing.

"Roman, baby, please don't leave me," I kiss his forehead. "I'll be back. I'll find help, I promise." I unwillingly leave my husband to go find someone who can help us.

I climb back up the hill, collapsing onto the side of the road as an eighteen-wheeler narrowly misses me. He pulls over to the side of the road, and runs over to help. I cry frantically for him to help Roman, and after calling 911, he races down the embankment and pulls Roman from the wreck.

There is nothing I can do but watch on from the top of the road; watch for the ambulance and watch this god-send of an angel try and save my husband's life.

"I've got a pulse!" the Texan trucker hollers, sounding just as relieved as I feel.

I sink to my knees, tears of happiness falling freely down my face.

The ambulance arrives and both Roman and I are taken to the emergency room.

I call Nova as soon as we get there while

Roman is rushed into emergency surgery. On top of everything else, I fear he might shift uncontrollably while on the theatre table, but my concerns are eased when Nova tells me there are two surgeons specifically rostered on who deal with the pack members.

I breathe a sigh of relief, closing my eyes and resting in the hospital bed, waiting for our family to arrive. My mind wanders. Memories of Roman flash through my mind; our honeymoon, our first time, our wedding, our first kiss, vivid dreams… suddenly it goes blank and though I will my eyes open they stay shut, waiting, anticipating something more, and then I see it—us— Roman and I, together again, but somehow we are not the same as we are now. We are in another time, another place. The love I feel for him radiates just as strongly as it does in this era, though what catches my attention the most is that same urgency I've been feeling so frequently as of late. Before I can grasp any further insight, a familiar voice pulls me from this strange flashback and I am startled awake.

"Ella?" Nova's voice surrounds me, her hands clasped over mine.

I open my eyes and they fill with tears. How thankful I am to see her standing at my bedside.

"Roman?" I whisper hoarsely.

A gentle smile touches Nova's lips as a single tear escapes down her golden toned cheek.

"He's ok. He'll be out of surgery shortly," her words are soothing, but I find myself still desperately searching her eyes for more, something she might be keeping from me.

"Elle, you have to stop working yourself up. You have been in a major car accident, you need to keep calm and let your body rest. Roman will be fine."

My heartrate climbs as that pressing-urgency floods my system again. I shake my head.

"No, Nova, listen to me, something is wrong. I—I can feel it. There is something really wrong. I want to see him. Now. I need to see him now," I rip the IV out of my hand and the oxygen tube out of my nose. Nova's eyes widen in horror as my gown slips off my shoulders, making the many cuts and bruises very visible. She quickly wraps the blanket around me and holds my body against hers, her strength too intense to break free from.

I crumble, collapsing into her arms in a weeping mess. Dena and Paul step into my room at that moment, their sullen expressions shifting as they encounter my distressed state.

"Nova, what's going on?" Dena embraces me, replacing her daughter's arms with her own.

"Ella thinks there's something wrong with Roman." Nova murmurs quietly.

I nod, burying my face into Dena's chest. "I can feel it. Something isn't right." I sob gracelessly, fighting to fill my lungs with air at the same time.

The small room suddenly goes a deafening quiet, and through my tear-filled eyes, I see everyone glancing at me with dumbfounded expressions.

Dena snaps something at Paul and he disappears in the blink of an eye. All I can do is wait. Wait for news about Roman. Wait to see him. Wait for whatever this urgency is to make sense.

Dena lays me down, draping the knitted blanket over my bruised body, and softly smooths her hand over my hair. Soon enough I am fighting an unwinnable battle against my heavy eyelids and I fall into a deep sleep.

I wake feeling a little disorientated. I have no indication of how many minutes or hours I was asleep for, but I am alone. The sun shines brightly through the large window that has its blind pulled down halfway, the shadows reflecting geometric shaped patterns on the walls. I look around the hospital room. Bouquets of flowers and get-well-soon cards line the tables and the windowsill. I search for the buzzer that summons the nurse and press the call button.

The absence of my family leaves a profound emptiness in my heart and I can't help but fear the worst. A short middle-aged nurse whisks into my room, a wide grin spreading across her chubby face.

"Good mornin'. How're you feelin' today?" she asks, bubbly as ever.

"I, um, I feel fine, thank you."

"I would hope so after that long sleep you just woke from." The nurse smiles over the clipboard she is holding.

"Long sleep?" I ask. "How long was I asleep for?"

"About a day and a half. But that's okay, love, your body needed it."

A day and a half?!

"Um, would you happen to know where my family are?" I ask anxiously.

The nurse takes a swift glance at her watch. "They should be arriving any minute now," she smiled her sweet smile. "Should we get that IV out of your arm and get you into the shower so you can be dressed and ready for when they arrive? You will be able to go home today."

I nod, forcing an appreciative smile, all the while only thinking about one thing, one person: my Roman.

"My husband, Roman Kahoa, has he been released yet?"

The nurse's smile slowly fades and she shakes her head.

"No, I'm sorry, dear, Mr. Kahoa was placed in an induced coma. I'm unsure as to why but I've heard they are wanting to try and see if he wakes up today."

"Thank you." I murmur, though I doubt whether she heard me, or perhaps it was more that I barely heard the words slip out of my mouth, and then I question whether I'd even said them to begin with.

The kind nurse helps me into the shower. The hot water cascades down my back as I sit on the shower floor, curled up in a ball. I knew exactly why Roman was placed into an induced coma. He must have been showing signs of shifting. The coma would have been more necessary for public safety than for his own. Either way, he needs me, that much is clear.

After my shower, I quickly dress, ignoring the minor aches and pains plaguing my body and I press the nurse to take me to see my husband.

As we approach his room, the nurse warns me that this sort of thing can be confronting. She offers to stay but I decline as politely as I can manage. She presses a green button on the wall to the left-hand side of the door and the door automatically opens into the room. I take a deep breath and step inside.

My eyes find him straight away. He is so still and peaceful in the too-small hospital bed. There aren't any tubes or anything— not at all what I imagined—but the confronting part is that he is so still, so quiet and peaceful, almost like... *No. Don't go there. He is alive. He is just sleeping,* my mind screams.

I take another breath and walk towards him. When I reach the edge of the bed I notice how much his wounds have already healed. Pink scars cover his face and his hands. I reach out, gently folding my hand over his.

"Roman? If you can hear me... I want you to know I'm here. I'm not going anywhere, okay? I love you." I pull up the blue leather chair that is leaning against the wall. Not releasing our hands, I sit, waiting an eternity it seems, to look into the eyes of my husband once more. I kiss the back of his hand and caress it softly as I rest my head on the edge of his bed and watch him intently as he sleeps.

Sooner than expected, the room fills with our entire immediate family. Everyone is here to witness their alpha being brought out of an induced coma—something that doesn't happen too regularly. The doctor rambles some medical mumbo-jumbo, though I am too excited to pretend to pay attention.

I watch on as he periodically reduces the

anesthetic. It takes longer than I envisioned.

It had been fifteen hours already and Roman was still not awake. Everyone was taking shifts staying with me when others went to find food and water whilst I refused to leave my husband's side.

"Roman, baby, you can wake up now. We are all so excited to see you," I smile, feeling the warmth in his hands becoming more intense and his color is almost back to normal. "Any time now." I tease him playfully, sounding impatient as ever, since I know how much he likes that.

Unexpectedly I feel Roman's hand tighten around mine.

"Oh my God! He just squeezed my hand! He squeezed my hand!" I jump up out of my seat.

"What?" Nova and Manti shoot up off their chairs so fast they both fly into the back wall.

"Manti, go get the doctor," Nova snaps frantically at her husband. "Elle will you be okay here while I go round everyone up?" her tone is calm and concerned all rolled into one. I can't take my eyes off of Roman, and though I am almost positive I replied out loud, I didn't actually hear my answer. I nod and within seconds Roman and I are alone again.

"Roman? Can you hear me?" I breathe, wishing more than anything to hear his voice whisper some sort of a reply.

Just as the door glides open and the doctor reappears, I feel Roman's hand gently hug mine once more. My heart fills with every intense emotion possible as the realization that my husband is coming back to me resonates, forcing me to ignore the unrelenting urgency that seems unwavering.

Manti and I step out of the room while the curly-haired doctor takes Roman's observations. I lean against the cool glass wall, sighing with relief.

"It won't be too much longer now, Elle." Manti wraps his arm around my shoulders, and we stay like that for a brief moment.

Nova, Dena and Mr. Kahoa, along with the rest of the pack jog up the corridor, excited grins stretched from ear-to-ear. Both Dena and Mr. Kahoa embrace me as soon as they are within arms-length of me. Then the doctor says the words we were all waiting so desperately to hear, no one more so than I.

"He is waking up." he says with a kind smile.

This is it. This is the moment we have all been waiting for. Suddenly I feel panicky. I need a minute to breathe and collect myself, so I allow everyone else to go in and sit with Roman first.

I take a few deep breaths, and by the third one the pull to be with Roman is far too intense to ignore for a second longer.

I take my place beside him, placing my hand over his and I wait for the grogginess to wear off.

Roman stirs as he comes out of the coma, but he smiles as soon as he sees his mom and the entire family surrounding him. It is the most heartwarming moment I have witnessed.

Emotions run rampant inside me for my husband, my eternal link. I want him to see me and smile my favorite smile.

His hand tightens around mine once more as he inhales deeply. His eyes find our hands entwined and he begins to search for me. As our eyes meet, my heart races a million miles a minute, almost seizing as his lips curl in at the corners and I fall in love all over again.

"Hi," he whispers softly.

"Hi," I smile back, tears escaping down

my cheeks. I hold his hand a little tighter, and as my vision clears from the flood of tears, I see how Roman is looking at me, his expression weary, unsure.

"Roman?" fear consumes every part of me. I have never seen him look at me like this. There is something really wrong here.

"Roman, you okay, darling?" Dena asks, stepping forward and taking his other hand.

His eyes never left mine, but they were empty, confused, yet searching for something or someone.

"Who are you?" he asks.

The wind is knocked out of me and my world slips away.

"Stop playing, Ro, that's your wife." I hear a familiar husky voice say from beside me. I can't look at him because if I do, I'll lose it. Instead, I keep my eyes focused on Roman, ignoring Kale's presence.

"My wife?" Roman sounds even more confused than before. "Where's Cheyenne?" he asks with his concerned voice.

I snatch my hand out of his and stand to my feet, my heart beating against my chest; anger, fear, love, and pain mixing into one terrifying cocktail as I search the room of shocked faces.

I can't be here. As hard as it is, I force myself to leave the room, pushing past Kale and the doctor as he re-enters the room. I walk as fast as my feet will go, though I feel as if I can't get away fast enough. And as I reach the nurses station, the kind chubby nurse who had helped me before chases after me as I head for the exit.

"Mrs. Kahoa? Mrs. Kahoa!" she called after me.

I stop as she pads over, my eyes fixed on the shiny floor.

"Mrs. Kahoa, I received your blood results from the lab and I was wondering if you knew that you were pregnant?" she murmurs gently, leaning in to keep our conversation as private as possible.

My eyes lift from the floor.

"I'm pregnant?" I whisper with utter confusion.

The nurse nods. "Yes, dear, you are."

I shake my head in disbelief. "No, there must be some mistake." I say as a single tear rolls down my already tear-streaked face.

"No mistake, Mrs. Kahoa. You are indeed pregnant, about six weeks or so according to your hCG levels,"

I nod, clasping my hand over my

stomach, and head for the exit.

"Congratulations." I hear the nurse call out, but I keep walking.

VII

∞

Weeks have passed, Roman is now home but not living with me; he is suffering with some form of Retrograde Amnesia. And since he doesn't remember me or anything about us, it seemed best for him to stay with his parents and in a place he was familiar with and in all honesty, it was a little easier for me to cope—at least I thought I was coping.

I hadn't left our home since the day it all happened. The only person I would allow over was Nova. She brought me food, not that I ate much, she washed my clothes, not that I would drag myself out of bed to change as often as I should, and she hugged me when I fell apart, which seemed to be all the time.

It had been about two days since Nova had last visited, and up until this point, I had been able to hide the fact that I was pregnant. My morning sickness is more of an all-day sickness, and it is violent! Eating actually scares me. Although, I remembered Lena had said she'd eat dry toast when she was pregnant with me, and that seemed to work for her. Desperate to look after the little jellybean in my stomach, I tried the plain toast theory, and to my surprise, it actually worked.

With my stomach settled, and the food actually staying down, I crawl back into bed. My bedroom window faces the Kahoa's home, and when sitting up in bed I can see Roman and Mr. Kahoa chopping wood by the side of the house. Roman looks happy, busy and focused, all the things I love about him. Hearing his laugh rips through me like a thousand knives, and I fall apart, crying relentlessly into his pillow.

As I lull, there is a knock at the front door. I have neither the strength nor the desire to open it, so I ignore the knocking.

Eventually it stops, but then I hear the door creak open and close softly. I assume Nova is back with more food. I stay where I am, curled into the fetal position on my bed, wrapped in the blankets that smell of Roman, and I close my eyes, praying to fall asleep to escape my painful reality.

The next thing I feel is the bed shift as the weight of somebody sitting on it startles me. My eyes flash open, and I see Kale beside me. My heart constricts and a surge of emotion gets the better of me. I sob into his chest as he wraps his arms around my body, consoling me the only way he knows how.

I can't lie. It feels *so good* to be held by someone so warm. I close my eyes and imagine it is Roman holding me, caressing my cheek, kissing my lips. Tears roll down my face and I pull away.

"Kale, I can't, this isn't right," I sigh.

"What's right anymore?" he breathes, his dark hair falling around the edges of his face. "You deserve to be happy and feel loved, Elle. I can give that to you." Kale's lips quirk up in true Kahoa fashion, his hand moving from my hair to my lips, wiping away the fallen tears.

"I still love *him*," I breathe, forcing back the wave of emotion threatening its way through.

"I know that, I love him too, but, Elle, he doesn't even remember who you are." His truthful words slice deeper through my already raw wounds.

"He is still *my Roman*. He is still every ounce of happiness I have ever known. I can't just forget that."

"I'm not asking you to forget what he means to you, Elle. All I am asking for is the chance to show you what you mean to me." Kale stares into my eyes, his emerald gaze compelling something deep and dark within me, but before I can act upon any of the feelings I am experiencing, I hear the one thing I never thought I would again. Cheyenne.

I run to the window and find Roman and Cheyenne sitting by the old oak tree with the swing. He is leaning against the tree trunk and she is curled around him, getting too close, and in a split second, he peers down at her and presses his lips to hers. Their kiss is my undoing. I lose it. Kale catches me as my knees buckle and I fall. He lays me back onto the bed and holds me close until my hysterical cries fall silent. He strokes my hair, caresses my cheek, and wipes away every tear that escapes my eyes.

"Why doesn't he remember who I am?" I force through the dryness of my throat.

"I don't know, Elle. You are what dreams are made of, I don't understand how he or anyone could forget you." He tucks a loose tendril of hair behind my ear and tilts my head back ever so slightly. Our eyes meet, and for the sake of not wanting to feel this pain anymore, I let Kale kiss me.

As his lips trail down my neck, every soft kiss brings a measure of comfort I had not expected. As much as I wished it was Roman kissing me right now, there was no guarantee that he would ever remember who I am, or what we once were to one another. I allow Kale to love me the way he has wanted for so long, and although it wreaks havoc on my mental and emotional stability, it gives me something else to focus on, something else to feel.

Lustful desire flares bright in his eyes, his resemblance to Roman spikes my temperature and sends my heart racing. The way his hands touch my body makes my skin sizzle. A passionate explosion takes hold as he parts my legs, lacing seductive kisses down my neck, grazing his teeth against my skin in gentle bites.

"I love you, Ella." He growls.

Sadness and heartbreak consume me as Kale utters those words. I push him away and sit upright against the headboard, placing considerable distance between us. Kale appears confused and alarmed by my sudden reaction.

"I'm sorry," I breathe, dropping my head into my hands. "I—I just can't."

Kale exhales loudly, then clearing his throat, he sits beside me.

"Did I do something wrong? Did I frighten you?" he asks, his voice soft.

"No, it's not that." I reply. After a momentary pause of silence, Kale speaks.

"It's just that I can hear your heartbeat. It's *fast*. In fact, I can hear *both* of your hearts beating, their rhythms almost the same fast pace,"

My head shoots up, my eyes fixed on Kale's.

"Does Roman know you're carrying his baby?"

I shake my head. "No."

Kale's hand folds over mine.

"I'm sorry. This was selfish of me." He waves his hand aimlessly over the bed.

"It wasn't entirely your fault, Kale. I just wanted to forget about him for a while. I was equally as selfish."

Kale shakes his head in disagreement. "Nah, you were just doing what you thought would help. Desperate times call for desperate measures, right?" he chuckles. "I promise not to try anything on you again unless it is what you really want."

"Deal." I force an appreciative smile.

"But I will be here for you. You need someone in your corner. Both of you do." He places our hands on my stomach.

Every day for the next week I would hear Cheyenne over at the Kahoa's. I couldn't bring myself to look out the window because I couldn't bear to see them together.

Nova came over to bring some more food. She put the groceries in the fridge and stood in the doorway with a disapproving look on her face.

"What?" I snap sourly.

"You need to get out of your pajamas

and get dressed. It's been weeks, Elle."

"What's wrong with what I've got on?"

"Nothing, they are totally cute, but they're starting to graft to your skin."

I make a face at Nova, and she challenges me with her own stubborn, equally as annoying face.

"Fine! I'll get changed." I storm into the bathroom and take a shower.

After dressing in some new clothes, I wander back out to the living room where Nova is patiently waiting.

"Feel better?" she asks, smug as ever.

"No." I lie. Her mouth curled into a knowing smile. She pats the sofa cushion beside her. I oblige, sitting next to her.

"Why is Cheyenne over at the house?" I ask, unable to refrain myself from asking the question, the elephant in the room. Nova shakes her head and exhales through her nose.

"She just showed up one day, I'm guessing she must have heard what had happened and decided to come see for herself."

"Yeah, but why hasn't anyone chased her off yet?" I ask, sounding more than annoyed.

"Elle, we are hoping she triggers his memory and he remembers who she really is and what she has done to him, us, and most importantly, to you. If she can make him remember who you are and what you are to him, she won't get a second look."

"Or kiss," I mumble under my breath.

"What?"

"I saw them kissing, again." I roll my eyes as the vision of Roman and Cheyenne kissing at Nova's wedding plagues my mind.

"Oh, Elle, I'm so sorry."

"Why couldn't it have been me? I would rather have been the one to be injured and be suffering with amnesia. At least then I would still have him." Tormenting heartbreak cripples me as I can do nothing but mourn the loss of my husband. Nova hugs me in her arms.

"Shh, I know this is hard, Elle. Have faith that everything will work out. You and Roman are eternally linked, nothing Cheyenne does can change that."

Those words were exactly true and the only thing I could hold onto to get through this nightmare.

The next few weeks were absolute hell. Not only was I suffering with the worst case of morning sickness in the history of pregnancy, but I was now beginning to show, and hiding my growing stomach from Nova was getting harder and harder with each passing day. And on top of everything, Cheyenne was constantly at the Kahoa's house.

Nova seemed to think she was keeping watch of Roman, just in case he happened to stumble over this way and regain some of his memory.

I knew she would be loving every minute of him not remembering who I am or what we are to each other. And then it occurred to me that she might have very well had something to do with the car accident.

"Are you actually watching this or is it watching you?" Kale's husky voice breaks my train of thought.

"Huh?" I look at him, confused. He grins and shakes his head, pointing at the TV.

"Oh. No I'm not really watching it. You can watch what you like." I toss the remote at him.

Kale had been coming over and spending time with me almost every other day. He cooked for me, held my hair back when I was throwing up, and helped keep Nova off the scent about my pregnancy.

Kale flicked off the TV and just as he was about to say something we hear *her*.

I throw my head back against the sofa and sigh loudly.

"You okay?"

"I can't handle much more of this. Can we just get out of here?"

"Sure." Kale smiles tenderly. He disappears into my bedroom and reemerges with one of Roman's big sweaters.

"Put this on. It will hide your bump."

I peer up at him with a grateful smile. "Thanks." I murmur, throwing on the oversized black knitted sweater.

As we head outside, the brisk air brushes coolly against my face and Roman's scent wafts through the breeze. Kale curls his arm around my waist, guiding me into the passenger seat of his SUV. For whatever reason, I felt the urge to look to my right and as I peek over my shoulder, I lock eyes with Roman who is sitting by the fire-pit across the way. Tears pool in my eyes, and the pain of having to leave my home because of him hurt more than words could describe. Roman looked away, dropping his eyes to the ground, and then Cheyenne came into view, stealing his attention.

"Come on, Elle, let's get you out of here." Kale's soft voice pulls me from the heart-aching daze and he helps me into the car. As we drive out of the driveway, I remember the last time Kale took me away from Roman, from this very place and in this very car. Cheyenne was involved then too. The distance felt like we were oceans apart, but just as we pulled out onto the tree-lined road, Roman catches my gaze once more and softly smiles. My heart almost launches out of my chest. It takes every ounce of strength I have to stay in the car, allowing the distance to increase inch by inch as we drive away.

Kale is still living in one of the long-term serviced apartments at the Featherbrook Hotel. Luckily the room he is in is a new one, I doubted whether I could have handled going back to the same one as last time.

Kale made us a light lunch while I played with his new photography equipment.

"You miss it?" he asks, crunching on a piece of carrot.

"Photography?" my voice scaled a few octaves higher than I intended. We both smile and I nod. "Yeah, I do actually."

"Why'd you give it up?"

I shrug my shoulders. "After Lena and Jack passed I sort of threw myself into wedding planning. I fully intended on going back to work fulltime, but then the wedding happened, and then the accident," I sigh. "Now I'm expecting and I would like to focus on him."

"Him? It's a boy?"

I beam brightly, cradling my baby bump. "I don't know for sure, but when I dream, I see a baby boy."

"That's pretty awesome. I bet you're right. You know, maternal instincts and all that." Kale grins, chomping into another carrot.

"Are you excited? You're going to be an uncle." I raise my eyebrows in suspense.

"Uncle Kale," he tried out his new title.

"'Tis got a nice ring to it. I like it."

'Me too." I agree.

We talked some more while we ate. Kale was careful with what he said and which direction our conversations took. We focused mainly on baby topics, which was really exciting and fun since I didn't have anyone else to talk to about it yet.

"Have you chosen names?" he asked cautiously.

"Mmhmm," I mutter, swallowing my food. I take a quick sip of juice and prepare myself emotionally to answer Kale's question. "I have my choice of names for both a boy and a girl."

"Ok, let's hear 'em."

"For a girl, I chose Delena Nova, after both of our moms and Nova. And for a boy, Roman Kale Jr, RJ for short. Obviously those names are self-explanatory." I fought back the tears that were harrowingly close to escaping.

"I really love both choices, Elle. And I'm really honored you chose to name your little one after me."

"Well, you're a big part of our lives, and you have always been there for me."

"I will always be here for you. You and your baby. There's nothing I wouldn't do for you, you know that, right?"

"I do, Kale. Thanks. You're a good friend. One of the best." I smile kindly. Looking at the clock, I realize the time. "I should really think about getting home. Would you mind driving me back?"

Kale glanced at the clock.

"I'll take you, but, first tell me something. Why would you go back there knowing you are subjecting yourself to all that pain watching Ro and Cheyenne?"

"I don't know… I guess I just need to be close to him."

"I get that, but, Elle, it's doing more harm than good."

As painful as it was, I knew he was right. I dropped my head into my hands feeling like such an idiot.

"Look, why don't you move in here with me?"

I glance up. "What?" I say, sounding a little too surprised.

Kale raises his hands in surrender. "Only until things get easier at home."

"Kale, that's a really generous offer, but don't you think it's a little too much? For you, I mean." Kale rolls his eyes and takes my hands into his.

"Because of my feelings for you, you mean?"

I nod and he smiles his dashing Kahoa smile that could melt the grandest of icebergs.

"All feelings aside, I would do this for you. We spend most of our time together anyway. It just makes sense for you to have a place you can escape to, especially now."

"Yeah, but asking someone to move in with you is a serious commitment."

"I am being serious. Look, I even have the face," he pulls a straight and serious facial expression and I can't help but laugh. "Come on, I promise you won't regret it. I will even let you have full control of the TV remote."

I sigh and stand to my feet. "Fine, yes, okay. But *only* until things get easier at home!" I warn, and Kale bows playfully.

VIII

∞

Nova had asked why I was staying away from my own home and when I told her I couldn't handle being there and seeing Roman with Cheyenne, she promised to make it right. I didn't quite know how to take that as she didn't elaborate, but if Nova said she was going to try and fix the situation, then I believed her.

Living with Kale had been a lot easier than I initially anticipated. He has grown so much from the guy I first met, although his feelings for me have also grown, and that has been extremely evident. Despite that, he has been really great about keeping them under control. I guess I am overly observant and aware.

It had been two weeks since I moved in, and whilst it has been painful being away from Roman, the time away has been good for me. But sadly, all things must come to an end; Kale just received a gig back in Canada and he is leaving in less than an hour.

He dragged his suitcase full of clothes behind him as I pack the last of my clothes.

"I know this sucks, but you think you'll be alright?" Kale met my eyes, and I saw the concern in his as he saw the startled expression on my face.

I turned away and zipped up my bag.

"Hey," Kale turned me to face him. "Everything will be okay."

"Yeah, but what if it's not?" I complain.

"We will deal with it then. Nova will be there with you. I know she will look after you. Probably a lot better than I can, but don't tell her I said that," He smiled and pulled me into him, wrapping his big arms around me. "I heard the old man chief is going to be there, too, so you will have someone else on your side," Kale chuckled darkly. "I wouldn't be surprised if he chased Cheyenne off. I'd pay to see that. Keep your phone handy, just in case you need to record anything for me." His eyes were alight with humor, making me laugh.

Back home, I noticed the fire blazing wildly in the fireplace as I walked into the house.

"Hello?" I called out, hesitating by the front door. I waited and after no reply I closed the door.

I sat by the fire, reveling in its warmth. A flood of memories swam inside my head, but before they got the better of me, a firm knock at the door snapped me back to reality.

I scaled to my feet and opened the timber door.

"Hello my darling," Grandpa stood, smiling back at me. All I could do was fall apart and cry as he embraced me. "Come now," he whispered, "Let's get inside where it is warmer." Never letting go, he closed the door behind us and sat with me by the fire.

"I am so happy to see you, you have no idea," I sobbed, wiping my tears on the oversized sweater of Roman's that I seemed to live in. "Everything has been such a mess since the car accident, Grandpa."

"I know, darling. That is why I have come. Nova sent word about everything going on over here while I have been away. I made it my first priority to come and be with you."

"Have you seen Roman?" I asked.

"Yes, I saw him. I probably didn't handle that as well as I could have. But he will get over it." Grandpa smiled warmly and chuckled under his breath. I wondered what he was talking about.

"What happened?"

"Oh, I am just a silly overprotective fool. It's nothing for you to worry yourself over, dear." He curled his warm wrinkled hand around mine, a knowing smile touching his elderly face. "May I?" he reached his hand out over my belly, and once I nodded, he gently placed his hand on my bump.

I marveled at this man's wisdom and knowledge.

"How did you know?" I asked, surprise saturating my awed tone.

"You are glowing radiantly," he crowed.

I gave him my I-don't-believe-you look and he laughed enthusiastically.

"Okay, okay," he took in a deep breath of air and held my hands. His face now serious, he began to speak. "There are a number of ways *I* know you are pregnant. Firstly, when you married Roman and consummated your marriage, you became the pack Chieftess, body and soul. As Chieftess, when expecting, a subtle golden glow emanates from right here," he traced his finger over my hairline and my forehead. "It has long been thought of as a crown as such, and only those with a trained eye can see it. Secondly, as alpha female, you smell like your alpha and Chief when expecting. You radiate a sweeter than normal aroma, Elle. If Roman wasn't suffering with amnesia, he would be extremely besotted by you, spellbound, even. In fact, it may be the very thing that helps his memory."

"Probably why Cheyenne has been keeping him on such a short leash." I scoff.

"Yes, well, I fear she had something to do with this whole ordeal."

"Really? Because I have had those very same thoughts!"

"Leave it with me. But you should be spending as much time with Roman as possible."

"That is easier said than done. That bitch won't leave his side," I growl. "I'm sorry, she just makes my blood boil."

"It is perfectly okay, my dear, I understand completely. You get some rest and leave everything to me." Grandpa smiled his Kahoa grin, kissed my cheek and gently pet my belly then left.

Being in his presence was so soothing for the soul. I felt calm and taken care of.

And as the night came to an end, I had a little something to eat and clambered into bed. I drifted to sleep counting the stars and listening to the tranquilizing chants coming from the tipi right outside.

As the sun rose, sun beams shone brightly in through the bay windows, though heavy clouds were visible in the distance, threatening to invade at any moment. I stepped out into the yard, the brisk breeze swirling and whipping my hair in its grasp. I inhaled deeply, allowing the sweet cherry-blossom scent that gave me butterflies to fill my entire being. Roman was close by. His delicious fragrance confirmed that much.

I fought with myself whether or not to seek him out and approach him, mostly out of fear of not seeing the love and devotion in his eyes that I had become so accustomed to, but also for the simple fact that I didn't want to see Cheyenne.

Short and quick wood splitting sounds echoed loudly, ending my pathetic brooding confliction. I followed the noise, rounded the house and caught sight of Roman chopping wood and stacking it along the side of the house.

Hiding behind the house, I peeked around the corner and simply watched as Roman picked up large logs, placed each one on the ground and hacked the wood in half and then quarters, placing the firewood in a neat pile. His muscles flexed and tensed with each maneuver, making distant memories of the two of us not so distant anymore.

Roman is in his ripped jeans and basketball jersey, he's all muscles, long hair, smelling divine, with burning dark eyes… burning dark eyes that are now locked with mine. My heart seizes and I want to hide but I can't move, I can't look away.

Roman drops the axe, and slowly moves toward where I stand half concealed by the house. His lips curl into a soft shy smile, my heart beating so fast it almost feels like it is in slow motion, and as Roman reaches the side of the house, he glances down at me, and my cheeks warm.

"Elle, right?" his voice is pure velvet. I nod, not yet able to find my words. Roman's smile widens, his eyes gliding to the moss covered ground and back up to me. "Sorry about all the noise," he points over his shoulder to the freshly chopped firewood. "The old man said you needed some firewood and kindling," he waited for me to say something, but I was amazed by his beauty and by how much this man could still affect me in ways no other ever could. "I can bring some of the wood inside if you want?" I nod again, and as he gathered some wood, I turned to head inside, feeling like the world's biggest idiot.

I didn't know what to do with myself. I fidgeted and fussed over the smallest things, moving pillows from one side of the sofa to the other, spritzing some perfume into the rooms and tidying as I went, and finally I checked my appearance in the mirror, pinching my cheeks for a more natural blush, not that I really needed it when Roman was around. I felt giddy, nervous, and on cloud nine all at once.

Roman walked in carrying two armfuls of firewood and carefully placed them by the fireplace, neatly stacking them where he had originally put our cut firewood when we first moved in.

He laughed silently and shook his head.

"What's wrong?" I ask without thinking. Roman turns to face me with a surprised look on his face.

"Ah, so she can speak." He teased, just like when we first met.

I smile involuntarily.

Roman turns back to the what he was doing and as he stacked the last piece of firewood in the woodpile, he added one to the dying fire, and watched as it roared to life. "I, uh... I feel as if I've done this before," he sounded so lost and confused. I on the other hand had to refrain myself from getting my hopes up too quickly. "It's like de ja vu or something." He laughs at his words, again shaking his head.

"There is a reason for that," I whisper, sitting on the sofa, staring at my knotted fingers.

From the corner of my eye I see Roman turn to face me.

I glance up at him, our eyes connecting. "You used to live here. You actually built this house." I watch as what I said registered within him. He glanced around the large living room, his eyes wide with wonder at what he had created and yet had no recollection of it.

"Why?" he asked. "Why did I build this house?" he ran his hand over the stone fireplace and its intricate detail.

My heart started to beat wildly as I contemplated how to answer his question.

"You, um, you built it for someone… someone you used to love very much." I force the words over the dry lump forming in my throat and fought against the emotion that wanted to surge out of me.

Roman caught my gaze, his eyes now glowing with something more intense, something I used to know. His hand touched mine, sending fierce electricity through my body. I gasp at the intensity of our bodies coming into contact, and I want nothing more than for him to remember me, pull me into his arms and make love to me right there on our living room floor. But instead, with his eyes full of admiration, he eagerly mutters: "Cheyenne?"

My heart wilts and my world shatters all over again. I pull my hand out of his and shake my head as hot tears pour down my face.

"I'm sorry," I sob. "I have to go." I run out of that house as fast as I can, hating the fact I am putting so much distance between us yet again. I run and don't stop until I reach the Kahoa's house and am in the arms of the old man. He holds me and lets me cry until I have nothing left to give.

Once I have settled somewhat, Roman's great grandfather makes us each a cup of hot chocolate, and we talk. He tells me that although it will be one of the hardest things I will ever have to go through, I have to be persistent with Roman. He thinks the more time I spend with him, the more Roman will remember. He says I need to be strong and remember that Roman isn't doing any of this to intentionally hurt me, and he thinks once Roman does regain his memory, he will hate himself for what he has put me through, which I also agree with.

Just as I am about to head back home in the hopes of catching Roman before he disappears, Cheyenne walks through the kitchen door. *I see red.* Grandpa clasps his hand over mine, pining me to the table. He stands to his feet, his age, along with anger making his frail body tremble.

"What are you doing here? You are not welcome here! Leave before I throw you out myself." He growls.

Cheyenne steps toward us, a smug grin plastered on her face. "Sit down old man. You wouldn't want to hurt yourself." Her eyes burn gaping holes in my head as she turns her stare on me. My body begins to shake and jolt uncontrollably. This feeling is one I recognize all too well. Grandpa places his arms around my shoulders, trying with all his might to calm me.

Cheyenne laughs wickedly. "At least one Kahoa man wants you. Too bad it isn't the one *you want*."

I launch at her, and she backs into the wall, fear written all over her face.

"Calm yourself, Ella. You can't let her get the better of you," Grandpa murmurs. *"You can't shift now."* He whispers, and I knew exactly why. I looked at him and I willed him to get Roman. Nobody else would be able to calm me down enough to stop me from shifting and I would be damned if Cheyenne would be the reason I would jeopardize my baby's life.

Cheyenne provoked and taunted me the second the old man left the room.

"If you know what's good for you, you will just disappear and let us live our lives." I snarl.

"You can live your life, Ella, and I will live mine with what's rightfully mine," she stepped closer. "Roman doesn't even know who you are anyway. You should really just cut your losses; don't you think?"

"No I don't, actually. In fact, I think you are the one who should cut her losses. See, you can play your little mind games, kill my parents, try and kill me, and cause as many car accidents as you want, but you will never be to Roman what I am. You will never be his eternal link." I seethe.

Cheyenne smiles and rolls her eyes. "So you worked it out. Good for you. It was supposed to be *you* in that car, not Roman! But it worked out perfectly for me. You're not dead, but he doesn't remember you. *You are as good as gone.* He is and will always be *mine*!" she growled.

"Except for one thing, Cheyenne. *Nothing* you do or say can change the fact that *his soul* is imprinted to *mine*, not yours." I smiled, flashing my teeth.

Cheyenne's hand flew up to my throat. She squeezed as hard as she possibly could, cutting off all oxygen to myself and my baby.

"No! Hey!" Grandpa Kahoa and Roman both ran in just as everything was fading and turning black and empty. I felt Roman catch my body as Cheyenne let go of my throat, and the old man snapped something in Qaletaqa at Roman. Without warning Roman and I are moving, and I fight to stay awake. I recognize a familiar hallway, a familiar room, and I am placed on a familiar bed. Roman murmurs something but it's too late, I'm fading into the darkness that is hell-bent on pulling me under, and I slip into unconsciousness.

IX

When I wake, Roman is lying next to me. I am on my side and I can see him watching me. I blink up at him, trying to fathom whether this is a dream or if I have really awoken to this moment, a moment I had only been able to relive in my wildest dreams.

Our eyes meet, and although we are shrouded in darkness, our thoughts and feelings masked, we are both very aware that we are looking at one another.

"Are you okay?" he asks, his voice gentle.

"I think so." I reply, captivated by his stare.

"I'm sorry," he whispers. "I am so sorry for everything," his eyes fill with tears, and my heart constricts. "Above everything, I am sorry I can't remember you." His tears fall unbidden. Unable to restrain myself, I enfold my body into his arms, consoling him, and his embrace soon tightens, holding me equally as securely to his body as I hold him to mine. "I want so much to remember you." He breathes.

Roman burrows his face into my hair, breathing in my scent; one deep breath after another. As he leans back, I reach up and wipe away his fallen tears. I can feel our hearts beating as one, and with the amazed look in Roman's eyes, I know he too can feel our love song playing strong, connecting us now just as it has for centuries before.

We grew inches closer as the moment wore on, our hearts in sync, beating in rhythm as one. Slowly but surely I could feel it; the pull, the intimacy, the familiarity we had once shared so strongly. Roman's hand carefully curls around the nape of my neck, gently pulling me into him. Our eyes stay fixed on one another and in a wisp of time there was a fleeting moment where his eyes whispered everything I had longed to hear. I couldn't help but wonder if my mind was playing tricks on me or if part of him was beginning to remember me again.

My breath hitches just as our lips touch, fireworks exploding within the depths of my soul as our kiss deepens, and images of our lives together flash through my mind; centuries of our love story echoing what I already knew; this is our destiny, we are each other's destiny.

Roman pulls away, his eyes wide with amazement, love and recognition as he smiles down at me with *that smile.*

"Did you see that too?" he asked elatedly. I smile back at him, my heart swelling with hope.

The look in Roman's eyes said it all, he didn't want this moment to end, and neither did I. Despite this, nothing else was said for a long while, we simply stayed entwined, reveling in this magical moment.

I rested my head against his chest, listening to his heart's melody, growing warmer the longer I listened to its beat. Roman softly played with my hair, his lips regularly pressing against my head in reassuring kisses, kisses that promised he was coming back to me.

I tightened my arms around my Roman's body, holding him as securely to me as I could manage.

"I love you," I whispered into the moonlight, wondering if he had missed me as much as I had missed him for all this time.

"Yes," he murmured quietly. "I have missed you more than you will ever know, Elle. I am only sorry it has taken me this long to realize it."

"It wasn't your fault, Roman," I scoffed, snapping almost, instantly regretting it.

"What does that mean?" he asked, justified concern saturating his tone.

Squeezing my eyes shut, I scalded myself internally before telling Roman the truth about Cheyenne's part in all this. His eyes widened in shock, but then I saw the pieces come together and I knew he saw the bigger picture once again.

"It's late, I'll walk you home." Was all he said, cold as ever.

The moon was hiding behind a thick blanket of clouds as we walked across the way to our house, the wind picking up, blowing fallen leaves around us as we walked in silence to the front door.

I looked up at Roman when we reached the front porch, wondering if he was angry with me.

"Thank you for walking me home… and for tonight," I whispered. "Goodnight," I said quietly, turning, heading inside. Roman's hand grasped mine, twirling me around to face him.

"I love you, Elle," he breathed, leaning in, kissing my lips tenderly. "Goodnight."

I smiled, rolling my lips together in an effort to conceal the butterflies dancing within me, urging me to take him inside and show him what he's been missing, but I didn't, I reluctantly turned and headed inside alone, locking the door behind me.

Roman didn't notice as I stood at the bay windows, watching as he lingered on our porch for a while longer, smiling as he looked around at the house he had built for me. Realization clearly dawned on him about our earlier conversation about the house, making him hover by the front door, obviously wanting to make things right. But before I could get to the door and out onto the porch, he was walking away, heading straight towards Black Bear's Landing. I watched him until he completely disappeared into the far-off oak trees and the darkness that surrounded them.

X

The brisk morning air was cool on my skin as I made my way over to the Kahoa's to check if Roman had made it home. Some part of me knew that if he had, he would have come home to me by now.

Nova met me at the front door just as I was about to knock. Her eyes lit up and she threw herself around me, hugging me tightly.

"Where have you been, Ella? I've missed you!"

"I've missed you too." I smile, much to

Nova's surprise.

"You're smiling, what's going on?" she questioned with a suspicious grin.

We walked and talked, making our way back to my place. I filled her in about the drama with Cheyenne yesterday and about her involvement with the car accident, how it was meant to kill me, not Roman. Nova was furious and rightfully so. This left her a little confused as to why I seemed so much happier, so, I told her about the moment Roman and I shared, how he was slowly coming back to me.

"The power of our eternal links will always win out in the end." She marveled, happiness emanating from her.

"It's more than that, Nova," I said. "Roman and I have an unbreakable bond that is timeless, sure, but we also have something else linking us together." I smiled at Nova as she looked back at me, puzzled. I took in a deep breath, placed my hands over my belly and smiled.

"We're pregnant." I announced. Nova's jaw dropped with utter surprise, and tears filled her eyes.

"Oh, Ella!" she cried happily. "Does Roman know?"

"No, I haven't told him yet, so please keep this between us for now."

Nova squealed with excitement. "I swear I won't say a word… Ahhh! I can't wait to be an aunt!" She bounced in her seat, reached out her hand, hovering it over my belly.

"May I?" she asked, her excitement palpable.

"Sure." I smiled as she placed her hands on my little baby bump.

"Who else knows?" she asked as she poked at my belly, willing my little jellybean to kick back.

"You, the old man, and Kale."

"Kale knows?" she asked hesitantly.

"Yes," I nodded. "He guessed, actually. Well, he heard baby's heartbeat and I couldn't deny it,"

Nova smiled, focusing on my belly once more. "I completely understand why you wouldn't. This is the greatest gift you and my brother could ever be given," she looked up at me. "When are you planning on telling him?"

"Honestly? I don't know. I'm waiting for the right time, that perfect moment," I sigh. "After last night, I really thought this morning would be the right time, partly why I came over to the house this morning, but he hasn't come home yet so I don't know."

"Where did he go?" Nova asked.

I pursed my lips, breathing in sharply. "He headed toward Black Bear's Landing, I'm assuming to see Cheyenne."

"Deal with her, you mean." Nova grinned, her eyes dark.

"Let's hope so. She has caused enough carnage. I wish she would just disappear." I mutter.

Nova placed her hand over mine, squeezing it protectively. "Tell Roman, heck, tell everyone about this little bundle of joy and watch the pack come together to protect you and their future Chief or Chieftess. Cheyenne will have no hope of getting anywhere near you. And not only that, but Roman will change,"

"Change? In what way?" I ask curiously.

Nova shook her head. "You'll see." She smiled a knowing smile, making me wish Roman would walk through the door right now so I could tell him he's going to be a daddy.

∞

Nova headed off to work, though not before trying to stir up my jellybean and make him kick. No luck was had, but that only made her more determined than ever, making me promise to be home after work so she could come by and have some secret aunt time.

I showered and dressed, taking my time to do even the simplest of things. I wanted the day to go by as fast as possible so I tried to keep relatively busy.

By five o'clock, I had finished all the housework and even put some chicken soup on for dinner. And at five past five, there was a knock at the door.

My heart raced the closer I got to the door and the butterflies we dancing yet again. I reached for the door handle, took a deep breath and pulled open the timber door.

"Hey you,"

"Hey yourself." I forced over the disappointment that was taking over every part of me. I walked back into the kitchen, trying my best to hide the pain that came along with the disappointment that it was Kale walking through my door instead of Roman.

"You're glowing, Elle. You really look beautiful," Kale came up from behind, wrapping his arms around my shoulders. I turned in his arms, breaking his hold, forcing a friendly smile.

"Thanks," I said, pulling away.

Kale moved closer, taking one step towards me. "I've really missed you," his hand tucked a loose strand of hair behind my ear and he surprised me by leaning in and kissing the side of my mouth. I took another step back, trapping myself between him and the counter.

"Kale, stop. We need to talk."

Kale gracefully stepped away, allowing me to get some very much needed distance between us. I retreated to the living room, sitting beside the dying fire and waited for Kale to join me.

After a minute or so he sat beside me, his shirt was unbuttoned at the top, his hair messy, he smelled divine as always and his hand was resting on mine. There was no doubt that Kale was beautiful and he was loyal in every way I'm sure every woman wishes a man to be, but there was one problem; he wasn't Roman. I turned to face him, his emerald eyes already on me.

"Kale," I began.

"Wait, Elle," he inhaled deeply. "Before

you say anything, let me tell you one thing,"

"No, Kale, I really need to tell you this! Whatever we were or you think we are is over. Roman and I are slowly finding our way back to each other but that can't happen if we keep allowing ourselves to blur the lines," Kale didn't say anything, I paused to give him a moment to allow everything to sink in before continuing. "I appreciate everything you have done for me and I love how you love me, but, I am in love with Roman. I can't just ignore our connection."

"What about *our* connection?" he demanded desperately.

"Kale, our connection is something entirely different. I can't deny that we have one, I feel it too, you know that. But it isn't the same as what Roman and I have… what you and Cheyenne have."

"I don't love her!" he insisted.

"I understand that is how you feel, but, I don't know, maybe give it some time?"

"*No*," Kale shook his head. "Ella, I'm in love with *you*."

There was a moment of awkward silence until I was forced to utter my next words.

"I'm sorry, but my feelings don't go any more beyond friendship." My voice was small. I hated knowing I was hurting him, especially since he had been such a rock through all of the craziness.

"Friendship? Well, isn't that a good thing? Friendship is the best foundation for a solid relationship, right?"

I sigh involuntarily as I drop my head into my hands. "Yes, and that should be your approach with Cheyenne. You might see something in her that nobody else can, something good…" the words tasted bitter coming out of my mouth because I knew better than anyone that there was nothing good about that girl.

"No. Please, Elle, will you just consider it? You could learn to love me."

"You shouldn't have to settle for a relationship like that!" I raised my voice, my patience wearing thin.

"But I would… I would settle for that if it means I have you, Elle, don't you see?"

I stared incredulously into Kale's desperate and sincere eyes, knowing all too well how much he meant every word.

"Kale, I can't do that you. I can't do that to myself. If things were different, then maybe we would have a chance, but I can't be untrue to myself, or to you for that matter. I do love you, just not in the way you want me to. I'm sorry."

Kale kneeled at my feet, his eyes deeply searching mine, yet it felt like he was almost trying to compel me to love him.

"The woman I love is right in front of me and yet still so far away." Kale whispered, his hand caressing my cheek as a single tear fell down his caramel brown skin.

At the exact moment Kale stood to his feet, the front door swung open. Nova and Roman both walked in. Nova smiled politely at Kale and made her way over to sit next to me, but Roman's eyes were wild, cautiously watching Kale's every move as he backed away from me.

Kale headed out the front door, stopping at his brother's side. They stared each other down for an intense few seconds and then Kale put his hand on Roman's right shoulder.

"You are one *very* lucky man." He murmured and left all in the same breath.

"You okay?" Nova asked quietly. I nodded and smiled, then got caught in Roman's gaze. "Well, good. I was coming over to see how you're doing," she sang coyly. "And then I found this one walking over." She pointed at her brother. Roman and I smiled at one another, the intimacy lingering in the air. His eyes searched my body from top to bottom, his warmth forcing my cheeks to blush under his fixed stare, my heart rate picked up and his eyes became fervent.

"Mom called you," he told Nova.

"No she didn't," she made a face and began to argue with her brother. Roman gave her a look and she clicked.

"*Oh*, right. Ok, I'll be back lat—"

"Don't bother, we will come over there," he rushed his sister out the still open front door, never taking his eyes off me. "Bye." He closed the door behind her and padded over to where I was sitting.

"Hi," I smiled up at him. He said nothing, he simply fell to his knees, curled his arms around my body and dragged me into his lap.

"I. Love. You." He mouthed ever so deliciously. I felt my insides jump and do beautiful things as Roman's voice captured every part of my body and soul.

There was something different about him, something new. I looked into his eyes and I saw it; he knew I had something I wanted to tell him. I liked that he hadn't guessed or noticed yet as I really wanted to see his reaction when I told him.

"I love you more. So much more in fact that I am going to make you a daddy." I took Roman's hand and gently placed it on my baby bump. His eyes fell from mine to where his hand rested. He stared in awe, carefully caressing my belly, his lips curling into the most heartwarming smile I have ever seen. His eyes, full of tears, hesitantly left my belly and locked with mine, lingering.

"*You're pregnant*?" he whispered, barely audible. I nodded as tears of my own rolled down my face. "Is this really happening? We're going to be parents?"

We stared at each other for another moment, then I answered quietly.

"Yes. We are going to be parents." I cried tears of joy and Roman soon followed as we rejoiced in this beautiful and sacred moment, a moment I had feared would never come.

I thanked my lucky stars as Roman cradled me in his arms, one hand on my belly and the other holding me securely to his body.

"You never cease to amaze me, Elle. Your love and patience guided me back to you, your magic brought me out of the amnesia, and your beautiful body is carrying our child. You are the most magnificent woman I have ever known and I am so incredibly honored to call you my wife."

XI

∞

Roman added two more logs into the fire, watching as it slowly caught alight, blazing to life once again. He returned to my side, cradling me gently against his body, his fingertips tracing slow circles on my belly. We stayed like this for an immeasurable amount of time, Roman's warmth radiated against my skin as he held me a little tighter while I watched the dancing flames of the fire.

Roman kissed my forehead, then leaned closer and whispered into my ear.

"I remember this."

I smiled, looking up into his eyes,

realizing I was thinking the very same thing. I snuggled into his chest, and we watched the fire flicker and spark as the light rain became heavy sheets, hard against the windows.

I lifted my head off Roman's chest and looked at him with hot and hazy eyes. He brought my hand to his lips, softly brushing his lips against my fingers. Muscles I hadn't felt tighten in so long tingled and tensed with every touch of his kiss, feeling the months of separation dissipating into sexual desire.

With one quirk of his lips, Roman's shy smile was my undoing. We gave into every urge, touching each other in places we hadn't in too long, reacquainting ourselves with our bodies.

Roman kissed my ear, my neck, my chest, the wet imprint of his lips lingering wherever his lips touched. He knelt back onto his knees, his face aglow in the firelight as his eyes watched me watch him pulling his shirt off, then his jeans. He slowly but gently lowered himself, hovering inches above me, his long ebony hair falling over us, shielding us from the world. I unbuttoned my blouse, slowly, intentionally trying to tease him. As the last button was unfastened, Roman slid his hand inside, his warm hand exploring my body, pushing the cotton fabric away from my skin, baring my breasts and my baby bump.

Roman stared in awe and amazement as his eyes traced the soft curves of my new body.

"Damn, baby, you are more beautiful than I remember." He breathed, barely above a whisper.

Unable to control himself any longer, Roman leaned in, running his tongue over and between my breasts, up my neck until our heated bodies finally pressed together.

His lips parted mine as he carefully lifted my hips, peeling off my leggings and panties. His tongue coaxed mine as his hand skimmed down my thighs, between my legs and he positioned himself into place. His skin copper, glowing in the blush of the soft fire.

Roman's breathing picked up, our bodies both trembling with anticipation. I bit into my bottom lip, stifling a shy smile, and it was in that moment that Roman and I became one.

His muscles tensed as he moved above

me, into me, and I cried in pleasure, hearing his as I watched him, captivated by his beauty and by how much he wanted me. He pushed into me, deeper, harder, and I felt his love, his strength, his soul. I let him control the journey, taking me to places I had only ever heard of. And with every deep breath, every moan of pleasure, all my fears and concerns slipped away, vanishing into thin air. Roman whispered sacred promises as we made love, as we kissed, and as we reached the climax, our bodies trembled in unison, and we collapsed in exhaustion, arm in arm.

Throughout the night, we followed a pattern of making love and lying in each other's arms, gazing into one another's eyes. Roman would softly sing me to sleep, or play with my hair until his warmth enveloped me and effectively pulled me into a wonderful dreamland like the world's best anesthesia.

There were moments where I would wake before Roman and he would still be fast asleep. I would savor those moments, watching him and thinking to myself how very lucky I was.

Roman would not always be as asleep as he appeared, listening to my thoughts, catching me by surprise when he would open his eyes and smile at me as he would watch me watch him, each of us looking at the other, thankful we were here in this moment, together at last.

As the sun began to rise, Roman and I made love once more. In the moments afterwards, I tried to tell him how happy I was, but he would have none of it. Instead, each time I tried to speak, he would kiss my lips, gently, lovingly, to keep me from saying a word. I fell in love with him all over again; his playfulness, his love and adoration for me.

When Roman had decided it was time to be serious, his expression shifted from playful to passionate. "Ella, I will never be able to apologize enough for leaving you for as long as I did. Amnesia is no excuse. You are my every dream, my every prayer answered. You are the reason I live every day. Your love, your faith, and your strength are what have helped me survive every storm, every failure, and every trial thrown my way. In this life and in every life I will love and cherish you, Ella Kahoa. More than you will ever be able to imagine. I promise you this."

Words had escaped me. I knew to do nothing else but allow the tears that were swimming in my eyes to fall. I pulled my husband into me so we could hold each other as closely and as tightly as we could.

I swore to myself in this moment that nothing nor no one would ever separate us ever again. Especially not *her*.

XII

∞

After breakfast, Roman and I headed over to the main house to announce our news.

I went inside first. Nova, Manti and Dena embraced me as I entered the kitchen. Shortly after, Mr. Kahoa lazily sauntered in wearing his robe and his moccasins, his face instantly brighter when he saw me standing in his kitchen.

"Now, here is a sight for sore eyes," he chuffed, beaming brightly as he almost leaped towards me. "How we have missed your smiling face around here, my dear." He pulled me into his arms, squeezing me tightly.

"You look beautiful, Elle." Nova grinned a knowing smile.

"You are positively glowing, darling. I have missed you so much." Dena wrapped her arms around me and held me tightly, kissing my cheek as she pulled away. I was careful to keep enough separation between us so they wouldn't feel my swollen belly.

At the very moment Dena pulled away, Roman walked in through the back door, startling everyone except Nova and I. We shared a fleeting look, a coy smile, and put our plan into action.

Everyone stared at Roman and then their eyes slowly drifted over in my direction. Nobody knew what to think or what to say.

"Good morning everyone," Roman finally said, his voice steady, giving nothing away.

"Good morning, darling," his mother stammered, not noticing her daughter's telling smile as she walked past her to hug her son. "Are you hungry? Would you like a cup of cocoa?" she asked Roman, then quickly turned to me. "Ella?" she asked, almost pleading. I shook my head with a polite smile, staying silent.

Dena was clearly feeling uneasy, unsure of what to say or do or what to make of the situation, especially when Roman kissed his mother's head and walked towards me.

The room was completely silent as our family watched on, unsure of what was happening or what to expect next. To be fair, I was also a little unsure of what to expect, and if past experience has taught me anything, I knew Roman well enough to know he more than likely wouldn't stick to our agreed upon plan, and it certainly was looking that way.

Roman winked playfully, a wicked grin touching his lips. He now stood right before me, our eyes locked on one another. He lifted his hands to my face, cradling either side, and kissed me.

We both smiled as we heard the sharp gasps around the room, ending our kiss, but staying arm in arm.

"Is this—does this mean what I think it does?" Dena asked full of excitement.

Roman and I looked at one another and smiled again. He nodded.

"Yes," he said, then paused. "But there is more to it now. Things have… changed." He announced.

Dena didn't know whether to smile or be concerned, her expression somewhere in between.

"Well of course things have changed, Roman, you couldn't remember anything about your life for a long time."

"No, no, it's not that," he shook his head, straight faced and suddenly serious. Everyone in the room had their eyebrows raised, even Nova wasn't so sure of herself anymore, but I sensed where Roman was going with this. "I am remembering more and more every second I spend with my wife, it's just…"

"What? What is it Roman?" Mr. Kahoa asked, his voice echoing concern.

"Things will never be the same again," he said, his voice shaking. A single tear drifted down his cheek as he placed his hand over my growing belly.

We both looked at each other and then at our family who were watching intently, eyes wide, tears rolling down their cheeks.

"Ella is pregnant." Roman announced proudly through his teary-eyed performance. Nova threw her head back in relief, glad we weren't dropping a bombshell she didn't know about, and Dena's face gradually

gained back some of her color as she
registered our news. Her red-rimmed eyes
spilled with happy tears, and Mr. Kahoa
pulled both Roman and I into him, holding
us as he wept with joy at the news of
becoming a grandpa.

After the shock of the news was behind us,
we were finally able to celebrate properly.
Mr. Kahoa and Manti organized the biggest
party since our wedding, inviting all of our
extended family and the pack members.
Roman and I were able to retreat to our quiet
little house whilst the preparations for the
party were underway.

My mind reeled at how excited everyone
was about our pregnancy. I never doubted
for a second that our baby wouldn't be loved
or doted on by everyone, but I just never
understood the strength or the intensity of
love and excitement everyone would feel
and express for our little jellybean.

I was suddenly struck with a sharpness
in my heart as my mind went to my parents.
They were the ones above every other who I
wanted to share this exciting news with. I

wanted to see their faces when Roman announced I was pregnant. I wanted to feel their arms around us and see their tears of joy at their wish of becoming grandparents finally coming true.

Now lying on our bed, Roman curled himself around me, holding me tenderly, listening to my thoughts as I fought back the overwhelming urge to cry.

"I wish they were here too," he whispered gently. I felt his smile against my ear. "I can just picture Jack spoiling our children with anything and everything they want, even when we say no." we both laugh at the thought. "He would have been the best grandfather, even more so than my father. Teaching them our history, our values and our beliefs. Our sacred obligations, how to shift, and how to control shifting," he pondered that for a moment and smiled. "I think my mom has even bigger shoes to fill. Lena would love our children like no one else could ever possibly dream of loving them. She would be their safe haven, their home away from home. Just like she was for you," he breathes, kissing my cheek as he gently turns me onto my back to face him. He nods as he stares into my eyes. "My parents have their work cut out for them. Don't get me wrong, I know they will do everything within their power for our children, they will love them and guide them, but I think even they know deep down that they will never be able to love our children the way your parents would."

I smile at how easily it is to accept everything Roman is saying. My parents were most certainly one of a kind. I feel so much happiness for having had the time with them that I did, but it hurts deeply that my children wouldn't get that chance.

"I promise that we will talk about Lena and Jack so much that our children will think they have known them."

"You keep saying that,"

"What?"

"'Our children'. Does that mean you want more than one?"

Roman smiles then and it touches his eyes. "I'd be happy with a whole football team," he jokes, at least I hope he's joking.

"We might need a bigger house." I point out sarcastically.

"I'll be sure to get right on it," he whispers, leaning in.

"Let's just focus on baby number one

for now, okay?"

"Sure, whatever you want," he presses his lips to mine. Pulling away slightly he looks at me all amazed. "I really love you." He murmurs, folding his arms around me.

"I really love *you*. Now, can we get some food because our little jellybean is hungry."

Roman and I walked back to the main house where the party was beginning to kick off in true Kahoa style. The whole pack was there, waiting for us to grace them all with our presence, but in all honesty I think they were all more excited about our little jellybean.

I peeked up at Roman as we walked across the yard. He held his head high, proud as ever, his arm around my waist and the biggest smile on his face. I wondered what the reason was behind his mischievous grin, but before I could figure it out Nova swept in and almost carried me off in her arms as she pushed me to the side, all secretive and serious. She stared at me, all the color draining from her face right before my eyes.

"God, Nova, you're scaring me. What is it?" I asked in a hushed tone.

"Kale is inside," she whispered, swallowing loudly. "And he has something to tell you." A cold shiver ran down my spine and both Nova and I looked toward the house. Instinctively I knew that whatever it was he wanted to tell me, mustn't be good.

XIII

∞

It was absolutely silent as I walked into the kitchen of the main house. Kale stood leaning against the island in the center of the room. Our eyes connected as I made my way towards him and his lips quirked up in his crooked smile.

"Hey you," he murmured, leaning down kissing my cheek.

"Hi." I reply, shocked by how unrecognizable my voice sounds. "Nova said you wanted to tell me something?"

"Yeah," he nods. "I'm surprised she didn't follow you."

"She's right outside looking out for

Roman. Just tell me what you came here to say and then we can both go about our business."

A light laugh escaped his lips. "Roman is welcome to join us, Elle. This does affect him too."

"Stop with the games, Kale. Just tell me what it is that you want to say and then you can leave." my voice was a lot louder than I had intended, but the frustration was getting the better of me.

Kale raised his hands in surrender, and moved to take a seat at the dining table. "You might want to sit down for this." He said, his voice strangely echoing concern.

I sat down across from him, careful to keep distance between us and I watched as he slowly became serious.

"After you made your decision to be with Roman I took your advice and tried to see how things would go with Cheyenne," he spoke softly, his eyes focused on mine.

"That's great." I reply. Kale shrugged his shoulders and made a face. "No? Not great? What happened?"

He inhales deeply, holding his breath for a few seconds, contemplating his next words it seemed. "Things were going okay, we were getting along fine enough, but then she told me she was pregnant."

I sit back in my chair, confusion swimming inside my head. "H—how can she be pregnant? You two only just…" my words fade as realization hit hard like a ton of bricks. My heart sinking in my chest.

Kale reached out across the table, his hand almost touching mine when the sliding door slams into the frame and Roman storms in like a wild, untamed beast.

He says nothing, he simply stares at Kale. I, on the other hand, couldn't bring myself to look up at either of them.

"Ella?" I heard Roman whisper my name but I ignore him, choosing to leave the room rather than subjecting myself to their impending standoff.

I make my way home. I feel all eyes on me as I avoid the gathering of family who are all there celebrating Roman and I and our unborn child. Little do they know they should be celebrating two unborn Kahoa babies.

After locking myself away in my house for

at least an hour, a soft tapping at the front door steals my attention. I roll off the couch and crack the door open just enough to see who is on the other side. Mr. Kahoa is standing there with a plate of food.

"May I come in?" he asks gently.

I push the door open and allow him to come inside. He thoughtfully closes the door behind him and sits beside me on the couch.

We sit in silence for a while, each of us picking at the mountain of food on the white platter sitting between us. And at some point as I poke at a piece of marinated chicken with my fork, imagining it is Cheyenne's head, I realize my father in-law has been watching me intently, probably trying to figure out whether I am going to snap and lose it or not. His voice is soft when he finally speaks.

"My dear. I can never apologize enough for the torment you are forced to endure all because of your love and connection to my son. But I also feel an obligation to remind you that there is nothing that could ever really break your bond with Roman. It doesn't matter how much Cheyenne or anyone tries to convince you otherwise; you know this within yourself, Ella. You just need to use the power of your link with Roman to illuminate the eternal bond you share. You are far more powerful than you believe, and Cheyenne suspects this, hence her continuous mind games. She is trying to break you." He pauses momentarily, then takes my hand in his. "Ella, just between you and I, legend has it that eternal links can be broken in one of two ways; the first is when the elders all seek the approval of the universe to have the link severed after it has been proven one half of the link is dark or life-threatening. And the other is when the woman chooses to sever the link." He looks into my eyes. "Ella, you have that power, that ability and that right as not only Roman's eternal link but also as his Chieftess."

I look at my father in-law, shock, awe and many other emotions coarse through my veins in this moment. But one thing I knew to be true was regardless of whether Cheyenne was telling the truth about being pregnant or not, there was no way she would succeed in coming between Roman and I.

"Thank you," I said, but before I could continue he shook his head and smiled.

"Don't thank me just yet. Roman has

been waiting outside to come in and talk to you."

"Oh he has, huh?" I smirk, though my heart races internally, not knowing whether seeing him right now is the right thing to do. My throat tightens as the front door slowly opens and he steps into the room.

As soon as our eyes meet, I realize how much I love him.

"Well, I'll get out of your way and let you two talk." Mr. Kahoa says, his voice trailing off as he stands and walks over to his son. "Be good to her." He says sternly with a pat on Roman's shoulder and closes the door behind himself once more as he leaves us alone.

I watch Roman as he looks back at me, and I see in his eyes that he knows how I feel about what Kale told me. He doesn't move and he doesn't say anything, he simply lowers his eyes to the floor and I find myself wondering what he is thinking.

I push myself up off the couch, and I waddle over to my husband. I gently wrap my hand around his and I squeeze softly. His eyes lift, searching for mine, and as soon as they lock, there is no doubt in my mind that Cheyenne is lying.

Roman opens his mouth to reassure me of the same, but I stop him, placing my finger over his lips.

"Shh," I whisper. "I know."

Roman folds his arms around me and laces my lips with his promising kiss.

I feel his warm smile curl his lips and my instincts suddenly begin to broil deep within. I know exactly what it is that I need to do, but first, I must distract Roman.

XIV

∞

Roman and I eventually made our way back over to the party which was being thrown in our honor. We mingled and watched one another carefully as some of the pack claimed Roman's attention and as Nova claimed mine.

Just as I saw the perfect opportunity to begin to put my plan into action, Logan pulls me aside.

"Hey," he smiled, his green eyes sparkling against the crackling fire that was blazing beside us. He quickly took my hand and tugged me to a quiet spot just beyond the trees.

"Hi. Wait, where are we going? Oh, you're not going all rogue too, are you?" I joke, referring to his brother.

He chuckles lightly. "No," he stops then and becomes serious, which is very unlike him. He is very much the playful one of the pack—next to Roman of course. "I just wanted to tell you something," he said ominously.

"God, what?" I reply, unable to keep any distress out of my tone.

"It stays between us." He cautions.

"Sure, of course. Logan, what is it?"

"Look, Ella. I know Kale told you Cheyenne is pregnant. And I know she is implying it is Roman's to get under your skin. But trust me, Roman never *ever* went there with her… not like that."

"How can you be so sure?" I ask.

"I'm sure. Roman told me she would try, but he couldn't do it. He said it felt like he was cheating on someone. It felt wrong to him so he never entertained the idea with her."

I felt the weight of the world lift from my shoulders. But just as I began to thank him, he said there was more.

"I don't care who she's been messing around with, there's no way she can be pregnant either."

"Really? Why not?" I ask, sounding intrigued.

Logan's shoulders slump as he breathes a deep breath. "I know because when I first began shifting, my hormones were all over the place and one night I was out hunting and came across her... one thing led to another and, well, you know..."

"Ew. Really?" I blurt out without thinking.

Logan shakes his head in disgust. "I know, I know. I'm not proud of it. But rumors went around that she was pregnant and I'm pretty sure she was the one who started them. But her brother Heath was the one who told me she can't get pregnant. Some abnormality or something. The point is, it is impossible for her to be pregnant because they never slept together and she couldn't get pregnant even if she tried. Everything she is doing is to hurt you and come between you and Roman. She's an evil piece of work, Elle."

"Tell me about it," I say, rolling my eyes. "I figured she was owed a little visit from yours truly."

"Oh yeah? When are you going?"

"Now. Could you do me a favor?"

He smiled a wicked smile, compelling mine. "Keep Roman occupied?" he asked with amusement.

"Yes please."

"You two are as bad as each other. Last time Roman made me babysit you and now you're asking me to babysit him."

"Hey! It's all part of the pack code. It says so right in the handbook." I joked and we laughed.

"Indeed. Well, you know I couldn't say no even if I wanted to. Just promise me something?"

"Sure."

"Be careful. And if you need me…" he tapped on his head.

"Wolf telepathy, got it." I said.

I hugged Logan a little tighter then and as I stepped out of his embrace he smiled playfully.

"Go get 'er." He growled.

As I disappeared into the dense forest, I took

one last look at my husband who was now sitting by the fire, laughing his musical laugh, with not a single care in the world. He was happy. And that's exactly how I wanted to remember seeing him.

The truth was, I didn't know how this was going to end. I felt it was best Roman be unaware of my plan. I had to do this, and if he knew of it, he would stop me. I couldn't risk it. Cheyenne needed to understand once and for all that she and Roman would never happen. And it needed to come from me.

EPILOGUE

∞

I finally reach the last dark forest fringed path that leads to Cheyenne's front door. I hammer at the heavy wooden door until she drags it open.

"Well, well, well, look what we have here. Where's Roman? I do have some brilliant news to share with him."

"Cut the crap Cheyenne! Everyone knows you're not pregnant." I snarl.

Cheyenne steps out of her house, a big dirty smile stretched across her face.

"Well, believe what you want, Ella. It's Roman's opinion I care about."

"He doesn't believe you either. In fact, he is certain you're lying. You see, in order to get pregnant, you need to have sex. And it's my understanding he wouldn't touch you. As a matter of fact, you're welcome to keep trying, but I'm fairly certain now that his memory has come back and he remembers what a troublemaking, desperate, ugly *bitch* you are, you wouldn't stand a chance with him." I smile in her face, and enjoy watching as her face begins twitching with fury.

"You would be wise to watch how you speak to me, half-breed." Cheyenne spat in my face. "You have more to lose than I do." She sneered, glancing down at my belly.

"Damn straight I do. Much more. And I will fight to the death to protect everything and everyone I have. So the next time you decide to threaten my unborn child's life, remember the laws you are bound by, and the consequences of breaking those laws. Or you could end up as one very unlucky puppy." I warn, turning away from her and heading back down the dirt path.

"He will hate you for risking his child's life like this!" she yelled through the trees. I stop and turn around to face her. She is halfway up the path to me now.

"*My* husband. *Our* child. That is *my* problem to deal with."

"Sure. I'm just putting it out there. You know, in case you've forgotten how protective he is."

My blood begins to simmer and I'm seeing red.

"I know *very* well how protective my husband can be. It seems you are the one who regularly forgets that fact."

"Oh, I don't forget, I just don't care. I could kill you and your little half-breed baby right here and now, and I would have Roman all to myself." She gloated.

"Yeah, for all of three seconds before he tears you to shreds!"

"Let's put that theory into play then, *shall we*?" she snarls.

"Go ahead!" I roar, launching myself towards her. "Do it! At least then Roman will kill you and we will both be rid of you!"

Cheyenne stepped back as she began to shift. My body also followed suit, trembling and shaking as I began to shift to protect both myself and my family. As Cheyenne burst into a big ball of white fur, I felt my spine crack, my eyes blurred as black and white spots claimed my vision.

"Ella, no!" I heard growled from behind me. It was Logan. He catches me just as I begin to fall to the ground, water trickling down my legs.

"Oh, God. Ella, your water broke." He says with horror.

His words enough to stop my body from continuing the motions of shifting forms. Instead, my body goes into survival mode. And just as Logan and I begin to climb off the forest floor, Cheyenne saunters toward us, teeth bared. Logan trembles as his body instinctively starts to shift in order to protect my jellybean and I.

The sudden shock on Cheyenne's face amuses me, but it doesn't last long as Roman leaps over Logan and I in wolf form, snapping at Cheyenne's throat as he rolls over her, throwing her into a tree.

Logan comes to, snapping out of shifting and gathers me up off the ground. He carries me into the forest, trying to find somewhere safe to hide.

I look back, hearing only the wild and savage sounds of two wolves trying to kill each other.

"You should have let me shift. I would

have killed her." I growl, struggling futilely to squeeze into the cave like shelter Logan had found in a large mossy tree trunk. His face soured.

"You probably would have killed yourself and the baby if you completely shifted. And Roman would have killed *me*." He looked at me, his eyes softening as he sees the fear of my reality in my face.

"I'm sorry." Is all I can choke out before I am riddled in pain with excruciating contractions.

Logan slides down the tree trunk, the look of fear prominent in his eyes.

"Ella, what can I do?" he questions frantically.

I can't answer. The contractions are hitting hard and fast, almost continuously, I don't even have time to get a full lungful of air.

I shake my head, implying there is nothing he can do. I start focusing on my breathing as images of Roman flash wildly through my mind.

"R-Ro," I pant, the pain taking my breath away.

"What? What is it?" Logan asks.

"Roman?" I force between breaths.

Logan shakes his head. "He'll be okay, Elle. Just keep breathing. I'm here, okay? I won't let you do this on your own." He squeezes my hand, sealing his promise just as I feel the urge to push.

"I want to push." I cry. Logan winces, his head snapping to the opposite direction as a low growl surrounds us.

"Shh." He whispers, pointing behind us. "There's a wolf." He mouths so quietly I had to read his lips to make out what he'd said. My heart races and the pain keeps building as another contraction blazes across my belly. I try to hold my breath. Logan clasps his hand over my mouth in an effort to stop me from screaming.

The wolf is getting dangerously close, and I doubt I can keep up quietly suppressing the agony tearing through my body. Logan hears my thoughts, his eyes flash widely at me, my belly, then outside. He wraps his arms around my trembling body, hugging me tightly and as my whimpering turns into a full blown blood curdling howl of pain, Logan throws himself out into the trees, shifting all in the same breath. Sacrificing his own life for mine.